THE FAIRY TALE
TREASURY

RAYMOND BRIGGS

THE FAIRY TALE TREASURY

Selected by Virginia Haviland

A YEARLING BOOK

Published by
Dell Publishing Co., Inc.
1 Dag Hammarskjold Plaza
New York, New York 10017

Yearling ® TM 913705, Dell Publishing Co., Inc.

ISBN: 0-440-42556-5

Reprinted by arrangement with Coward, McCann Inc., a division of the Putnam Publishing Group

Printed in the United States of America

One Previous Edition

December 1986

10 9 8 7 6 5 4 3 2 1

WAK

Contents

SARA CONE BRYANT

The Gingerbread Boy

Once upon a time there was a little old woman and a little old man, and they lived all alone in a little old house. They hadn't any little girls or any little boys, at all. So one day, the little old woman made a boy out of gingerbread; she made him a chocolate jacket, and put cinnamon seeds in it for buttons; his mouth was made of rose-coloured sugar; and he had a gay little cap of orange sugar-candy. When the little old woman had rolled him out, and dressed him up, and pinched his gingerbread shoes into shape, she put him in a pan; then she put the pan in the oven and shut the door; and she thought, "Now I shall have a little boy of my own."

When it was time for the Gingerbread Boy to be done she opened the oven door and pulled out the pan. Out jumped the Gingerbread Boy on to the floor, and away he ran, out of the door and down the street! The little old woman and the little old man ran after him as fast as they could, but he just laughed, and shouted –

"Run! run! as fast as you can!

"You can't catch me, I'm the Gingerbread Man!"

And they couldn't catch him.

The little Gingerbread Boy ran on and on, until he came to a cow, by the roadside. "Stop, little Gingerbread Boy," said the cow; "I want to eat you." The little Gingerbread Boy laughed, and said –

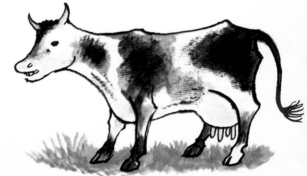

"I have run away from a little old woman,
"And a little old man,
"And I can run away from you, I can!
"Run! run! as fast as you can!
"You can't catch me, I'm the Gingerbread Man!"
And the cow couldn't catch him.

The little Gingerbread Boy ran on, and on, and on, till he came to a horse, in the pasture. "Please stop, little Gingerbread Boy," said the horse, "you look very good to eat." But the little Gingerbread Boy laughed out loud. "Oho! Oho!" he said –

"I have run away from a little old woman,
"A little old man,
"A cow,
"And I can run away from you, I can!"

And, as the horse chased him, he looked over his shoulder and cried –

"Run! run! as fast as you can!
"You can't catch me, I'm the Gingerbread Man!"
And the horse couldn't catch him.

By and by the little Gingerbread Boy came to a barn full of threshers. When the threshers smelled the Gingerbread Boy, they tried to pick him up, and said, "Don't run so fast, little Gingerbread Boy, you look very good to eat." But the little Gingerbread Boy ran harder than ever, and as he ran he cried out –

"I have run away from a little old woman,
"A little old man,
"A cow,
"A horse,
"And I can run away from you, I can."

And when he found that he was ahead of the threshers, he turned and shouted back to them –

"Run! run! as fast as you can!

8

"You can't catch me, I'm the Gingerbread Man!"
And the threshers couldn't catch him.

Then the little Gingerbread Boy ran faster than ever. He ran and ran until he came to a field full of mowers. When the mowers saw how fine he looked, they ran after him, calling out, "Wait a bit! Wait a bit, little Gingerbread Boy, we wish to eat you!" But the little Gingerbread Boy laughed harder than ever, and ran like the wind. "Oho! oho!" he said –

"I have run away from a little old woman,
"A little old man,
"A cow,
"A horse,
"A barn full of threshers,
"And I can run away from you, I can!"

And when he found that he was ahead of the mowers, he turned and shouted back to them –

"Run! run! as fast as you can!
"You can't catch me, I'm the Gingerbread Man!"
And the mowers couldn't catch him.

By this time the little Gingerbread Boy was so proud that he didn't think anybody could catch him. Pretty soon he saw a fox coming across a field. The fox looked at him and began to run. But the little Gingerbread Boy shouted across to him, "You can't catch me!" The fox began to run faster, and the little Gingerbread Boy ran faster, and as he ran he chuckled –

"I have run away from a little old woman,
"A little old man,
"A cow,
"A horse,
"A barn full of threshers,
"A field full of mowers,
"And I can run away from you, I can!

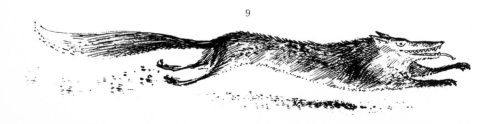

"Run! run! as fast as you can!

"You can't catch me, I'm the Gingerbread Man!"

"Why," said the fox, "I would not catch you if I could. I would not think of disturbing you."

Just then, the little Gingerbread Boy came to a river. He could not swim across, and he wanted to keep running away from the cow and the horse and the people.

"Jump on my tail, and I will take you across," said the fox.

So the little Gingerbread Boy jumped on the fox's tail, and the fox swam into the river. When he was a little way from the shore he turned his head, and said, "You are too heavy on my tail, little Gingerbread Boy, I fear I shall let you get wet; jump on my back."

The little Gingerbread Boy jumped on his back.

A little farther out, the fox said, "I am afraid the water will cover you, there; jump on my shoulder."

The little Gingerbread Boy jumped on his shoulder.

In the middle of the stream the fox said, "Oh, dear! little Gingerbread Boy, my shoulder is sinking; jump on my nose, and I can hold you out of the water."

So the little Gingerbread Boy jumped on his nose.

The minute the fox got on to the shore he threw back his head, and gave a snap!

"Dear me!" said the little Gingerbread Boy, "I am a quarter gone!" The next minute he said, "Why, I am half gone!" The next minute he said, "My goodness gracious, I am three-quarters gone!"

And after that, the little Gingerbread Boy never said anything more at all.

JOSEPH JACOBS

Henny-Penny

One day Henny-Penny was picking up corn in the cornyard when – whack! – something hit her upon her head. "Goodness gracious me!" said Henny-Penny, "the sky's a-going to fall; I must go and tell the king."

So she went along and she went along, and she went along till she met Cocky-Locky. "Where are you going, Henny-Penny?" says Cocky-Locky.

"Oh! I'm going to tell the king the sky's a-falling," says Henny-Penny.

"May I come with you?" says Cocky-Locky. "Certainly," says Henny-Penny. So Henny-Penny and Cocky-Locky went to tell the king the sky was a-falling.

They went along, and they went along, and they went along till they met Ducky-Daddles. "Where are you going to, Henny-Penny and Cocky-Locky?" says Ducky-Daddles.

"Oh! we're going to tell the king the sky's a-falling," said Henny-Penny and Cocky-Locky.

"May I come with you?" says Ducky-Daddles. "Certainly," said Henny-Penny and Cocky-Locky. So Henny-Penny, Cocky-Locky, and Ducky-Daddles went to tell the king the sky was a-falling.

So they went along, and they went along, and they went along, till they met Goosey-Poosey. "Where are you going to, Henny-Penny, Cocky-Locky, and Ducky-

12

Daddles?" said Goosey-Poosey.

"Oh! we're going to tell the king the sky's a-falling," said Henny-Penny and Cocky-Locky and Ducky-Daddles.

"May I come with you?" said Goosey-Poosey.

"Certainly," said Henny-Penny, Cocky-Locky, and Ducky-Daddles. So Henny-Penny, Cocky-Locky, Ducky-Daddles, and Goosey-Poosey went to tell the king the sky was a-falling.

So they went along, and they went along, and they went along, till they met Turkey-Lurkey. "Where are you going, Henny-Penny, Cocky-Locky, Ducky-Daddles, and Goosey-Poosey?" says Turkey-Lurkey.

"Oh! we're going to tell the king the sky's a-falling," said Henny-Penny, Cocky-Locky, Ducky-Daddles, and Goosey-Poosey.

"May I come with you, Henny-Penny, Cocky-Locky, Ducky-Daddles, and Goosey-Poosey?" said Turkey-Lurkey. "Oh certainly, Turkey-Lurkey," said Henny-Penny, Cocky-Locky, Ducky-Daddles, and Goosey-Poosey. So Henny-Penny, Cocky-Locky, Ducky-Daddles, Goosey-Poosey, and Turkey-Lurkey all went to tell the king the sky was a-falling.

So they went along, and they went along, and they went along, and they went along, till they met Foxy-Woxy; and Foxy-Woxy said to Henny-Penny, Cocky-Locky, Ducky-Daddles, Goosey-Poosey, and Turkey-Lurkey, "Where are you going, Henny-Penny, Cocky-Locky, Ducky-Daddles, Goosey-Poosey, and Turkey-Lurkey?" And Henny-Penny, Cocky-Locky, Ducky-Daddles, Goosey-Poosey, and Turkey-Lurkey said to Foxy-Woxy: "We're going to tell the king the sky's a-falling."

"Oh! but this is not the way to the king, Henny-Penny, Cocky-Locky, Ducky-Daddles, Goosey-Poosey, and Turkey-Lurkey" says Foxy-Woxy. "I know the proper way; shall I show it to you?" "Oh, certainly, Foxy-

Woxy," said Henny-Penny, Cocky-Locky, Ducky-Daddles, Goosey-Poosey and Turkey-Lurkey. So Henny-Penny, Cocky-Locky, Ducky-Daddles, Goosey-Poosey, Turkey-Lurkey, and Foxy-Woxy all went to tell the king the sky was a-falling.

So they went along, and they went along, and they went along, till they came to a narrow and dark hole. Now this was the door of Foxy-Woxy's cave. But Foxy-Woxy said to Henny-Penny, Cocky-Locky, Ducky-Daddles, Goosey-Poosey, and Turkey-Lurkey: "This is the short way to the king's palace; you'll soon get there if you follow me. I will go first and you come after, Henny-Penny, Cocky-Locky, Ducky-Daddles, Goosey-Poosey, and Turkey-Lurkey."

"Why of course, certainly, without doubt, why not?" said Henny-Penny, Cocky-Locky, Ducky-Daddles, Goosey-Poosey, and Turkey-Lurkey.

So Foxy-Woxy went into his cave, and he didn't go

very far, but turned around to wait for Henny-Penny, Cocky-Locky, Ducky-Daddles, Goosey-Poosey, and Turkey-Lurkey. At last Turkey-Lurkey went through the dark hole into the cave. He hadn't got far when "Hrumph," Foxy-Woxy snapped off Turkey-Lurkey's head and threw his body over his left shoulder. Then Goosey-Poosey went in, and "Hrumph," off went her head and Goosey-Poosey was thrown beside Turkey-Lurkey. Then Ducky-Daddles waddled down, and "Hrumph" snapped Foxy-Woxy, and Ducky-Daddles's head was off and Ducky-Daddles was thrown alongside Turkey-Lurkey and Goosey-Poosey.

Then Cocky-Locky strutted down into the cave, and he hadn't gone far when "Snap, Hrumph!" went Foxy-Woxy and Cocky-Locky was thrown alongside of Turkey-Lurkey, Goosey-Poosey, and Ducky-Daddles.

But Foxy-Woxy had made two bites at Cocky-Locky; and when the first snap only hurt Cocky-Locky but didn't kill him, he called out to Henny-Penny. But she turned tail and off she ran home; so she never told the king the sky was a-falling.

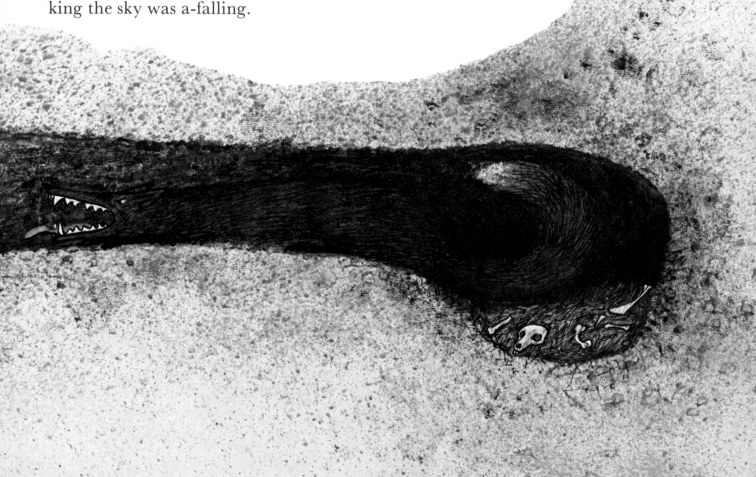

THE BROTHERS GRIMM

The Wolf and the Seven Little Kids

There was once on a time an old goat who had seven little kids and loved them with all the love of a mother for her children. One day she wanted to go into the forest and fetch some food. So she called all seven to her and said, "Dear children, I have to go into the forest; be on your guard against the wolf; if he comes in, he will devour you all – skin, hair, and all. The wretch often disguises himself, but you will know him at once by his rough voice and his black feet."

The kids said, "Dear mother, we will take good care of ourselves; you may go away without any anxiety." Then the old one bleated and went on her way with an easy mind.

It was not long before someone knocked at the house-door and cried, "Open the door, dear children: your mother is here and has brought something back with her for each of you."

But the little kids knew that was the wolf by the rough voice. "We will not open the door," cried they. "You are not our mother. She has a soft, pleasant voice, but your voice is rough; you are the wolf!"

The wolf went away to a shopkeeper and bought himself a great lump of chalk, ate this and made his voice soft with it. Then he came back, knocked at the door of the house, and cried, "Open the door, dear children, your

mother is here and has brought something back with her for each of you."

But the wolf had laid his black paws against the window, and the children saw them and cried, "We will not open the door; our mother has not black feet like you; you are the wolf!"

Then the wolf ran to a baker and said, "I have hurt my feet, rub some dough over them for me." And when the baker had rubbed his feet over, he ran to the miller and said, "Strew some white meal over my feet for me." The miller thought to himself, "The wolf wants to deceive someone," and refused; but the wolf said, "If you will not do it, I will devour you." Then the miller was afraid and made his paws white for him. Truly men are like that.

So now the wretch went for the third time to the house-door, knocked at it, and said, "Open the door for me, children, your dear little mother has come home and has brought every one of you something from the forest."

The little kids cried, "First show us your paws that we may know if you are our dear little mother."

The wolf put his paws in through the window, and when the kids saw that they were white, they believed that all he said was true and opened the door. But who should come in but the wolf! They were terrified and wanted to hide. One sprang under the table, the second into the bed, the third into the stove, the fourth into the kitchen, the fifth into the cupboard, the sixth under the washing-bowl, and the seventh into the clock-case. But the wolf found them and used no great ceremony; one after the other he swallowed them down his throat. The youngest in the clock-case was the only one he did not find. When the wolf had satisfied his appetite, he took himself off, laid himself down under a tree in the green meadow outside, and began to sleep.

Soon afterwards the old goat came home again from the forest. Ah! what a sight she saw there! The house-door stood wide open. The table, chairs, and benches were thrown down, the washing-bowl lay broken to pieces, and the quilts and pillows were pulled off the bed. She looked for her children, but they were nowhere to be found. She called them one after another by name, but no one answered. At last, when she came to the youngest, a soft voice cried, "Dear mother, I am in the clock-case." She took the kid out, and it told her that the wolf had come and had eaten all the others. Then you may imagine how she wept over her poor children.

At length in her grief she went out, and the youngest kid ran with her. When they came to the meadow, there lay the wolf by the tree and snored so loud that the branches shook. She looked at him on every side and saw that something was moving and struggling in his gorged body. "Ah heavens," said she, "is it possible that my poor children whom he has swallowed down for his supper can be still alive?"

The little kid had to run home and fetch scissors, and a needle and thread, and the goat cut open the monster's stomach. Hardly had she made one cut, before one little kid thrust its head out, and when she had cut farther, all six sprang out one after another. They had suffered no injury whatever, for in his greediness the monster had swallowed them down whole. What rejoicing there was! The kids embraced their dear mother, and jumped like a tailor at his wedding. The mother, however, said, "Now go and look for some big stones, and we will fill the wicked beast's stomach with them while he is still asleep."

The seven kids dragged the stones thither with all speed and put as many of them into the wolf's stomach as

it would hold. The mother sewed him up again in the greatest haste, so that he was not aware of anything and never once stirred.

When the wolf at length had had his sleep out, he got on his legs; and as the stones in his stomach made him very thirsty, he wanted to go to a well to drink. But when he began to walk and move about, the stones in his stomach knocked against each other and rattled. He cried out:

"What rumbles and tumbles
  Against my poor bones?
  I thought 'twas six kids,
  But it's nought but big stones."

When the wolf got to the well and stooped over the water and was just about to drink, the heavy stones made him fall in, and drown miserably.

The seven kids came running to the spot and cried aloud, "The wolf is dead! The wolf is dead!" and danced for joy round about the well with their mother.

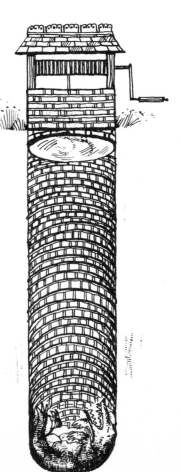

JOSEPH JACOBS

The Story of the Three Little Pigs

Once upon a time when pigs spoke rhyme
And monkeys chewed tobacco,
And hens took snuff to make them tough,
And ducks went quack, quack, quack. O!

There was an old sow with three little pigs, and as she had not enough to keep them, she sent them out to seek their fortune. The first that went off met a man with a bundle of straw, and said to him:

"Please, man, give me that straw to build me a house."

Which the man did, and the little pig built a house with it. Presently came along a wolf, and knocked at the door, and said:

"Little pig, little pig, let me come in."

To which the pig answered:

"No, no, by the hair of my chiny chin chin."

The wolf then answered to that:

"Then I'll huff, and I'll puff, and I'll blow your house in."

So he huffed, and he puffed, and he blew his house in, and ate up the little pig.

The second little pig met a man with a bundle of furze and said:

"Please, man, give me that furze to build a house."

Which the man did, and the pig built his house. Then along came the wolf, and said:

"Little pig, little pig, let me come in."

"No, no, by the hair of my chiny chin chin."

"Then I'll huff, and I'll puff, and I'll blow your house in."

So he huffed, and he puffed, and he puffed, and he huffed, and at last he blew the house down, and he ate up the little pig.

The third little pig met a man with a load of bricks, and said:

"Please, man, give me those bricks to build a house with."

So the man gave him the bricks, and he built his house with them. So the wolf came, as he did to the other little pigs, and said:

"Little pig, little pig, let me come in."

"No, no, by the hair on my chiny chin chin."

"Then I'll huff, and I'll puff, and I'll blow your house in."

Well, he huffed, and he puffed, and he huffed and he puffed, and he puffed and huffed; but he could *not* get the house down. When he found that he could not, with all his huffing and puffing, blow the house down, he said:

"Little pig, I know where there is a nice field of turnips."

"Where?" said the little pig.

"Oh, in Mr. Smith's Home-field, and if you will be ready tomorrow morning I will call for you, and we will go together, and get some for dinner."

"Very well," said the little pig, "I will be ready. What time do you mean to go?"

"Oh, at six o'clock."

Well, the little pig got up at five; and got the turnips before the wolf came (which he did about six), who said:

"Little pig, are you ready?"

24

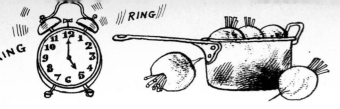

The little pig said: "Ready! I have been and come back again, and got a nice potful for dinner."

The wolf felt very angry at this, but thought that he could outwit the little pig somehow or other, so he said:

"Little pig, I know where there is a nice apple tree."

"Where?" said the pig.

"Down at Merry-Garden," replied the wolf, "and if you will not deceive me I will come for you at five o'clock tomorrow and get some apples."

Well, the little pig bustled up the next morning at four o'clock, and went off for the apples, hoping to get back before the wolf came; but he had farther to go, and had to climb the tree, so that just as he was coming down from it, he saw the wolf coming, which, as you may suppose, frightened him very much. When the wolf came up he said:

"Little pig, what! Are you here before me? Are they nice apples?"

"Yes, very," said the little pig. "I will throw you down one." And he threw it so far, that while the wolf went to pick it up, the little pig jumped down and ran home. The next day the wolf came again, and said to the little pig:

"Little pig, there is a fair at Shanklin this afternoon, will you go?"

"Oh yes," said the pig, "I will go; what time shall you be ready?"

"At three," said the wolf. So the little pig went off before the time as usual, and got to the fair, and bought a butter-churn, which he was going home with, when he saw the wolf coming. Now he could not tell what to do. So he got into the churn to hide, and by so doing turned it round, and it rolled down the hill with the pig in it, which frightened the wolf so much, that he ran home without going to the fair. He went to the little pig's house and

told him how frightened he had been by a great round thing which came down the hill past him. Then the little pig said:

"Hah, so I frightened you. I had been to the fair and bought a butter-churn, and when I saw you, I got into it, and rolled down the hill."

Then the wolf was very angry indeed, and declared he *would* eat up the little pig, and that he would get down the chimney after him. When the little pig saw what he was about, he filled his pot full of water, and made up a blazing fire. Just as the wolf was coming down, he took off the cover, and in fell the wolf. The little pig put the cover on again in an instant, boiled him up, and ate him for supper, and lived happy ever afterwards.

JOSEPH JACOBS

The Old Woman and Her Pig

An old woman found a crooked sixpence while sweeping her door-yard. "What shall I do with this sixpence?" she said. "I will go to the market and buy a pig."

Then the old woman went to the market and bought a pig. On her way home she came to a stile and then the pig would not go over the stile.
"Pig, pig, get over the stile,
Or I can not get home tonight."
But the pig would not.

Then she went a little farther and met a dog; and she said to the dog:
"Dog, dog, bite pig;
Pig won't get over the stile;
And I can not get home tonight."
But the dog would not.

Then she went a little farther and met a stick; and she said to the stick:
"Stick, stick, beat the dog;
Dog won't bite pig;
Pig won't get over the stile;
And I can not get home tonight."
But the stick would not.

Then she went a little farther and met a fire; and she said to the fire:
"Fire, fire, burn stick;

28

Stick won't beat dog;
Dog won't bite pig;
Pig won't get over the stile;
And I can not get home tonight."
But the fire would not.

Then she went a little farther and met some water; and she said to the water:
"Water, water, quench fire;
Fire won't burn stick;
Stick won't beat dog;
Dog won't bite pig;
Pig won't get over the stile;
And I can not get home tonight."
But the water would not.

Then she went a little farther and met an ox; and she said to the ox:
"Ox, ox, drink water;
Water won't quench fire;
Fire won't burn stick;
Stick won't beat dog;
Dog won't bite pig;
Pig won't get over the stile;
And I can not get home tonight."
But the ox would not.

Then she went a little farther and met a butcher; and she said to the butcher:
"Butcher, butcher, pen ox;
Ox won't drink water;
Water won't quench fire;
Fire won't burn stick;
Stick won't beat dog;
Dog won't bite pig;
Pig won't get over the stile;
And I can not get home tonight."

But the butcher would not.

Then she went a little farther and met a rope; and she said to the rope:
"Rope, rope, whip butcher;
Butcher won't pen ox;
Ox won't drink water;
Water won't quench fire;
Fire won't burn stick;
Stick won't beat dog;
Dog won't bite pig;
Pig won't get over the stile;
And I can not get home tonight."
But the rope would not.

Then she went a little farther and met a rat; and she said to the rat:
"Rat, rat, gnaw rope;
Rope won't whip butcher;
Butcher won't pen ox;
Ox won't drink water;
Water won't quench fire;
Fire won't burn stick;
Stick won't beat dog;
Dog won't bite pig;
Pig won't get over the stile;
And I can not get home tonight."
But the rat would not.

Then she went a little farther and met a cat; and she said to the cat:
"Cat, cat, bite rat;
Rat won't gnaw rope;
Rope won't whip butcher;
Butcher won't pen ox;
Ox won't drink water;
Water won't quench fire;

Fire won't burn stick;
Stick won't beat dog;
Dog won't bite pig;
Pig won't get over the stile;
And I can not get home tonight."

But the cat said to her, "If you will get me a saucer of milk, I will bite the rat." Then the old woman gave the saucer of milk to the cat and this is what happened:

The cat began to bite the rat; the rat began to gnaw the rope; the rope began to whip the butcher; the butcher began to pen the ox; the ox began to drink the water; the water began to quench the fire; the fire began to burn the stick; the stick began to beat the dog; the dog began to bite the pig; the pig got over the stile; and the old woman got home that night.

SARA CONE BRYANT (RETOLD FROM JOSEPH JACOBS)

The Little Red Hen and the Grain of Wheat

One day as the Little Red Hen was scratching in a field, she found a grain of wheat.

"This wheat should be planted," she said. "Who will plant this grain of wheat?"

"Not I," said the Duck.

"Not I," said the Cat.

"Not I," said the Dog.

"Then I will," said the Little Red Hen. And she did.

Soon the wheat grew to be tall and yellow.

"The wheat is ripe," said the Little Red Hen. "Who will cut the wheat?"

"Not I," said the Duck.

"Not I," said the Cat.

"Not I," said the Dog.

"Then I will," said the Little Red Hen. And she did.

When the wheat was cut, the Little Red Hen said, "Who will thresh this wheat?"

"Not I," said the Duck.

"Not I," said the Cat.

"Not I," said the Dog.

"Then I will," said the Little Red Hen. And she did.

When the wheat was all threshed, the Little Red Hen said, "Who will take this wheat to the mill?"

"Not I," said the Duck.

"Not I," said the Cat.

32

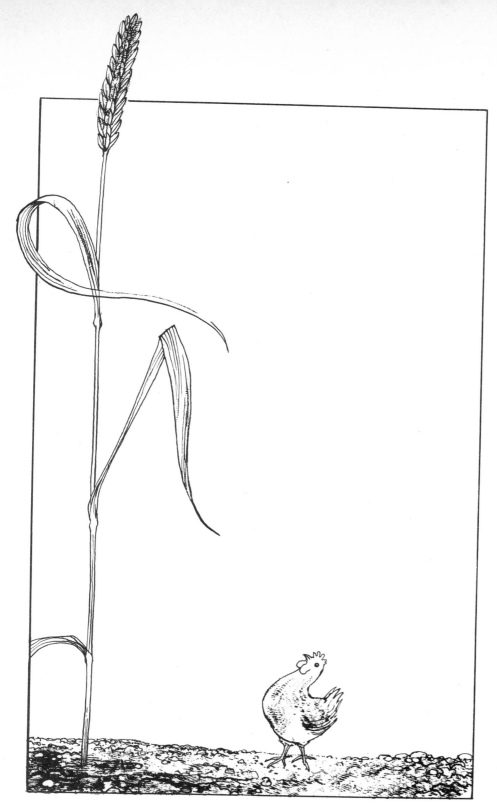

"Not I," said the Dog.

"Then I will," said the Little Red Hen. And she did.

She took the wheat to the mill and had it ground into flour. Then she said, "Who will make this flour into bread?"

"Not I," said the Duck.

"Not I," said the Cat.

"Not I," said the Dog.

"Then I will," said the Little Red Hen. And she did.

She made and baked the bread. Then she said, "Who will eat this bread?"

"Oh! I will," said the Duck.

"And I will," said the Cat.

"And I will," said the Dog.

"No, No!" said the Little Red Hen. "I will do that." And she did.

ROBERT SOUTHEY (RETOLD BY FLORA ANNIE STEEL)

The Story of the Three Bears

Once upon a time there were three Bears, who lived together in a house of their own, in a wood. One of them was a Little Wee Bear, and one was a Middle-sized Bear, and the other was a Great Big Bear. They had each a bowl for their porridge; a little bowl for the Little Wee Bear; and a middle-sized bowl for the Middle-sized bear; and a great bowl for the Great Big Bear. And they had each a chair to sit in; a little chair for the Little Wee Bear; and a middle-sized chair for the Middle-sized Bear; and a great chair for the Great Big Bear. And they had each a bed to sleep in; a little bed for the Little Wee Bear; and a middle-sized bed for the Middle-sized Bear; and a great bed for the Great Big Bear.

One day, after they had made the porridge for their breakfast and poured it into their porridge-bowls, they walked out into the wood while the porridge was cooling that they might not burn their mouths by beginning too soon, for they were polite, well-brought-up Bears. And while they were away, a little girl called Goldilocks, who lived at the other side of the wood and had been sent on an errand by her mother, passed by the house and looked in at the window. And then she peeped in at the keyhole, for she was not at all a well-brought-up little girl. Then seeing nobody in the house she lifted the latch.

The door was not fastened, because the Bears were good

36

Bears who did nobody any harm and never suspected that anybody would harm them. So Goldilocks opened the door and went in; and well pleased was she when she saw the porridge on the table. If she had been a well-brought-up little girl she would have waited till the Bears came home, and then, perhaps, they would have asked her to breakfast; for they were good Bears – a little rough as is the manner of Bears, though for all that very good-natured and hospitable. But she was an impudent, rude little girl, and so she set about helping herself.

First she tasted the porridge of the Great Big Bear, and that was too hot for her. Next she tasted the porridge of the Middle-sized Bear, but that was too cold for her. And then she went to the porridge of the Little Wee Bear, and tasted it, and that was neither too hot nor too cold, but just right, and she liked it so well that she ate it all up, every bit!

Then Goldilocks, who was tired, for she had been catching butterflies instead of running on her errand, sat down in the chair of the Great Big Bear, but that was too hard for her. And then she sat down in the chair of the Middle-sized Bear, and that was too soft for her. But when she sat down in the chair of the Little Wee Bear, that was neither too hard, nor too soft, but just right. So she seated herself in it, and there she sat till the bottom of the chair came out, and down she came, plump upon the ground, and that made her very cross, for she was a bad-tempered little girl.

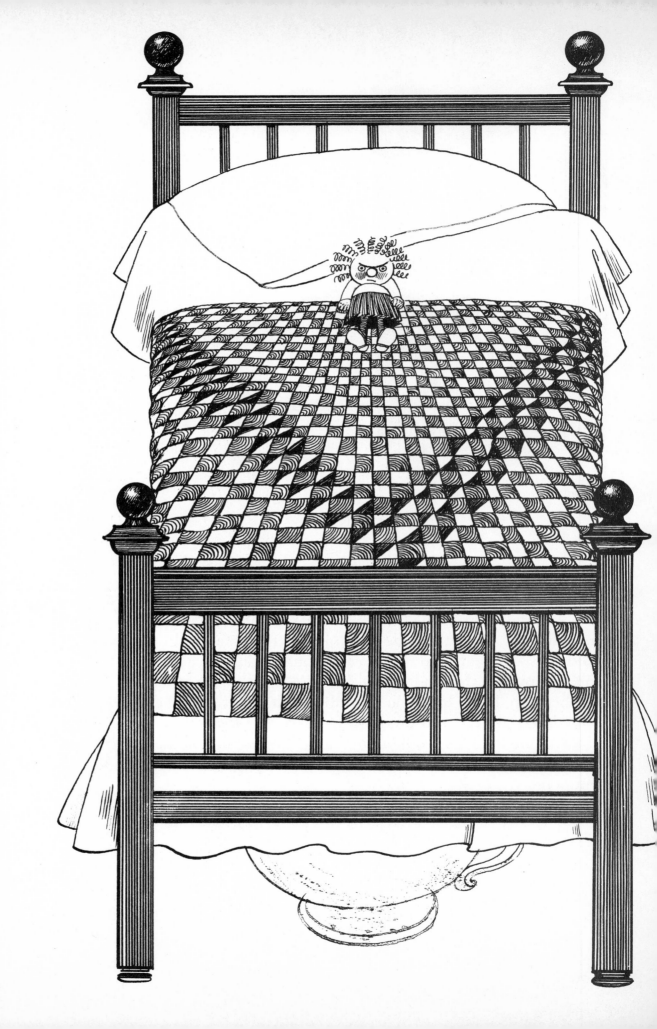

Now, being determined to rest, Goldilocks went upstairs into the bedchamber in which the Three Bears
slept. And first she lay down upon the bed of the Great
Big Bear, but that was too high at the head for her. And
next she lay down upon the bed of the Middle-sized Bear,
and that was too high at the foot for her. And then she lay
down upon the bed of the Little Wee Bear, and that was
neither too high at the head, nor at the foot, but just right.
So she covered herself up comfortably, and lay there
till she fell fast asleep.

By this time the Three Bears thought their porridge
would be cool enough for them to eat it properly; so they
came home for breakfast. Now careless Goldilocks had

41

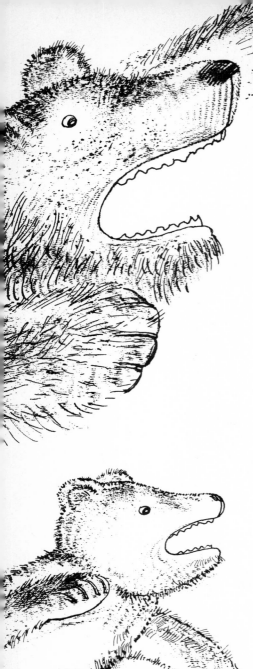

left the spoon of the Great Big Bear standing in his porridge.

"SOMEBODY HAS BEEN AT MY PORRIDGE!"

said the Great Big Bear in his great, rough-gruff voice.

Then the Middle-sized Bear looked at his porridge and saw the spoon was standing in it too.

"SOMEBODY HAS BEEN AT MY PORRIDGE!"

said the Middle-sized Bear in his middle-sized voice.

Then the Little Wee Bear looked at his, and there was the spoon in the porridge bowl, but the porridge was all gone!

"Somebody has been at my porridge and has eaten it all up!" said the Little Wee Bear in his little wee voice.

Upon this the Three Bears, seeing that someone had entered their house, and eaten up the Little Wee Bear's breakfast, began to look about them. Now the careless Goldilocks had not put the hard cushion straight when she rose from the chair of the Great Big Bear.

"SOMEBODY HAS BEEN SITTING IN MY CHAIR!"

said the Great Big Bear in his great, rough, gruff voice.

And the careless Goldilocks had squatted down the soft cushion of the Middle-sized Bear.

"SOMEBODY HAS BEEN SITTING IN MY CHAIR!"

said the Middle-sized Bear in his middle-sized voice.

"Somebody has been sitting in my chair, and has sat the bottom through!" said the Little Wee Bear in his little wee voice.

Then the Three Bears thought they had better make further search in case it was a burglar; so they went upstairs into their bedchamber. Now Goldilocks had pulled the pillow of the Great Big Bear out of its place.

"SOMEBODY HAS BEEN LYING IN MY BED!"

said the Great Big Bear in his great, rough, gruff voice.

And Goldilocks had pulled the bolster of the Middle-sized Bear out of its place.

"SOMEBODY HAS BEEN LYING IN MY BED!"
said the Middle-sized Bear in his middle-sized voice.

But when the Little Wee Bear came to look at his bed, there was the bolster in its place!

And the pillow was in its place upon the bolster.

And upon the pillow – ?

There was Goldilocks' yellow head – which was not in its place, for she had no business there.

"Somebody has been lying in my bed – and here she is still!"
said the Little Wee Bear in his little wee voice.

Now Goldilocks had heard in her sleep the great, rough, gruff voice of the Great Big Bear; but she was so fast asleep that it was no more to her than the roaring of wind, or the rumbling of thunder. And she had heard the middle-sized voice of the Middle-sized Bear, but it was only as if she had heard someone speaking in a dream. But when she heard the little wee voice of the Little Wee Bear, it was so sharp and so shrill that it awakened her at once. Up she started, and when she saw the Three Bears on one side of the bed, she tumbled herself out at the other and ran to the window. Now the window was open, because the Bears, like good, tidy Bears, as they were, always opened their bedchamber window when they got up in the morning. So naughty, frightened little Goldilocks jumped; and whether she broke her neck in the fall or ran into the wood and was lost there or found her way out of the wood and got whipped for being a bad girl and playing truant no one can say. But the Three Bears never saw anything more of her.

ALEKSEI TOLSTOY

The Turnip

Once upon a time an old man planted a little turnip and said:

"Grow, grow, little turnip, grow sweet! Grow, grow, little turnip, grow strong!"

And the turnip grew up sweet and strong and big and enormous.

Then, one day, the old man went to pull it up. He pulled and pulled again, but he could not pull it up. He called the old woman.

The old woman pulled the old man,
The old man pulled the turnip.

And they pulled and pulled again, but they could not pull it up. So the old woman called her granddaughter.

The granddaughter pulled the old woman,
The old woman pulled the old man,
The old man pulled the turnip.

And they pulled and pulled again, but they could not pull it up. The granddaughter called the black dog.

The black dog pulled the granddaughter,
The granddaughter pulled the old woman,
The old woman pulled the old man,
The old man pulled the turnip.

And they pulled and pulled again, but they could not pull it up. The black dog called the cat.

The cat pulled the dog,

44

The dog pulled the granddaughter,
The granddaughter pulled the old woman,
The old woman pulled the old man,
The old man pulled the turnip.
And they pulled and pulled again, but still they could not
pull it up. The cat called the mouse.
The mouse pulled the cat,
The cat pulled the dog.
The dog pulled the granddaughter,
The granddaughter pulled the old woman,
The old woman pulled the old man,
The old man pulled the turnip.
They pulled and pulled again, and up came the turnip at
last.

WANDA GÁG

Gone Is Gone

This man, his name was Fritzl – his wife, her name was Liesi. They had a little baby, Kinndli by name, and Spitz who was a dog.

They had one cow, two goats, three pigs, and of geese they had a dozen. That's what they had.

They lived on a patch of land, and that's where they worked.

Fritzl had to plough the ground, sow the seeds and hoe the weeds. He had to cut the hay and rake it too, and stack it up in bunches in the sun. The man worked hard, you see, from day to day.

Liesi had the house to clean, the soup to cook, the butter to churn, the barn yard and the baby to care for. She, too, worked hard each day as you can plainly see.

They both worked hard, but Fritzl always thought that he worked harder. Evenings when he came home from the field, he sat down, mopped his face with his big red handkerchief, and said: "Hu! How hot it was in the sun today, and how hard I did work. Little do you know, Liesi, what a man's work is like, little do you know! *Your* work now, 'tis nothing at all."

"'Tis none too easy," said Liesi.

"None too easy!" cried Fritzl. "All you do is to putter and potter around the house a bit – surely there's nothing hard about such things."

48

"Nay, if you think so," said Liesi, "we'll take it turn and turn about tomorrow. I will do your work, you can do mine. I will go out in the fields and cut the hay, you can stay here at home and putter and potter around. You wish to try it – yes?"

Fritzl thought he would like that well enough – to lie on the grass and keep an eye on his Kinndli-girl, to sit in the cool shade and churn, to fry a bit of sausage and cook a little soup. Ho! that would be easy! Yes, yes, he'd try it.

Well, Liesi lost no time the next morning. There she was at peep of day, striding out across the fields with a jug of water in her hand and the scythe over her shoulder.

And Fritzl, where was he? He was in the kitchen, frying a string of juicy sausages for his breakfast. There he sat, holding the pan over the fire, and as the sausage was sizzling and frizzling in the pan, Fritzl was lost in pleasant thoughts.

"A mug of cider now," that's what he was thinking. "A mug of apple cider with my sausage – that would be just the thing."

No sooner thought than done.

Fritzl set the pan on the edge of the fireplace, and went down into the cellar where there was a big barrel full of cider. He pulled the bung from the barrel and watched the cider spurt into his mug, sparkling and foaming so that it was a joy to see.

But Hulla! What was that noise up in the kitchen – such a scuffle and clatter! Could it be that Spitz-dog after the sausages? Yes, that's what it was, and when Fritzl reached the top of the stairs, there he was, that dog, dashing out of the kitchen door with the string of juicy sausages flying after him.

Fritzl made for him, crying, "Hulla! Hulla! Hey, hi, ho, hulla!" But the dog wouldn't stop. Fritzl ran, Spitz

ran too. Fritzl ran fast, Spitz ran faster, and the end of it was that the dog got away and our Fritzl had to give up the chase.

"Na, na! What's gone is gone," said Fritzl, shrugging his shoulders. And so he turned back, puffing and panting, and mopping his face with his big red handkerchief.

But the cider, now! Had he put the bung back in the barrel? No, that he hadn't, for here he was still holding the bung in his fist.

With big fast steps Fritzl hurried home, but it was too late, for look! the cider had filled the mug and had run all over the cellar besides.

Fritzl looked at the cellar full of cider. Then he scratched his head and said, "Na, na! What's gone is gone."

Well, now it was high time to churn the butter. Fritzl filled the churn with good rich cream, took it under a tree and began to churn with all his might. His little Kinndli was out there too, playing Moo-cow among the daisies. The sky was blue, the sun right gay and golden, and the flowers, they were like angels' eyes blinking in the grass.

"This is pleasant now," thought Fritzl, as he churned away. "At last I can rest my weary legs. But wait! What about the cow? I've forgotten all about her and she hasn't had a drop of water all morning, poor thing."

With big fast steps Fritzl ran to the barn, carrying a bucket of cool fresh water for the cow. And high time it was, 'I can tell you, for the poor creature's tongue was hanging out of her mouth with the long thirst that was in her. She was hungry too, as a man could well see by the looks of her, so Fritzl took her from the barn and started off with her to the green grassy meadow.

But wait! There was that Kinndli to think of – she would surely get into trouble if he went out to the meadow. No, better not take the cow to the meadow at all. Better keep her nearby on the roof. The roof? Yes, the roof! Fritzl's house was not covered with shingles or tin or tile – it was covered with moss and sod, and a fine crop of grass and flowers grew there.

To take the cow up on the roof was not so hard as you might think, either. Fritzl's house was built into the side of a hill. Up the little hill, over a little shed, and from there to the green grassy roof. That was all there was to do and it was soon done.

The cow liked it right well up there on the roof and was soon munching away with a will, so Fritzl hurried back to his churning.

But Hulla! Hui! What did he see there under the tree? Kinndli was climbing up on the churn – the churn was tipping! spilling! falling! and now, there on the grass lay Kinndli, all covered with half-churned cream and butter.

"So that's the end of our butter," said Fritzl, and blinked and blinked his blue eyes. Then he shrugged his shoulders and said, "Na, na! What's gone is gone."

He picked up his dripping Kinndli and set her in the sun to dry. But the sun, now. It had climbed high up into the heavens. Noontime it was, no dinner made, and Liesi would soon be home for a bite to eat.

With big fast steps Fritzl hurried off to the garden. He gathered potatoes and onions, carrots and cabbages, beets and beans, turnips, parsley and celery.

"A little of everything, that will make a good soup,"

said Fritzl as he went back to the house, his arms so full of vegetables that he could not even close the garden gate behind him.

He sat on a bench in the kitchen and began cutting and paring away. How the man did work, and how the peelings and parings did fly.

But now there was a great noise above him. Fritzl jumped to his feet.

"That cow," he said. "She's sliding around right much up there on the roof. She might slip off and break her neck."

Up on the roof went Fritzl once more, this time with loops of heavy rope. Now listen carefully, and I will tell you what he did with it. He took one end of the rope and tied it around the cow's middle. The other end of the rope he dropped down the chimney and this he pulled through the fireplace in the kitchen below.

And then? And then he took the end of the rope which was hanging out of the fireplace and tied it around his own middle with a good right knot. That's what he did.

"Oh yo! Oh ho!" he chuckled. "That will keep the cow from falling off the roof." And he began to whistle as he went on with his work.

He heaped some sticks on the fireplace and set a big kettle of water over it.

"Na, na!" he said. "Things are going as they should at last, and we'll soon have a good big soup. Now I'll put the vegetables in the kettle –"

And that he did.

"And now I'll put in the bacon – "

And that he did too.

"And now I'll light the fire – "

But that he never did, for just then, with a bump and a thump, the cow slipped over the edge of the roof after all;

52

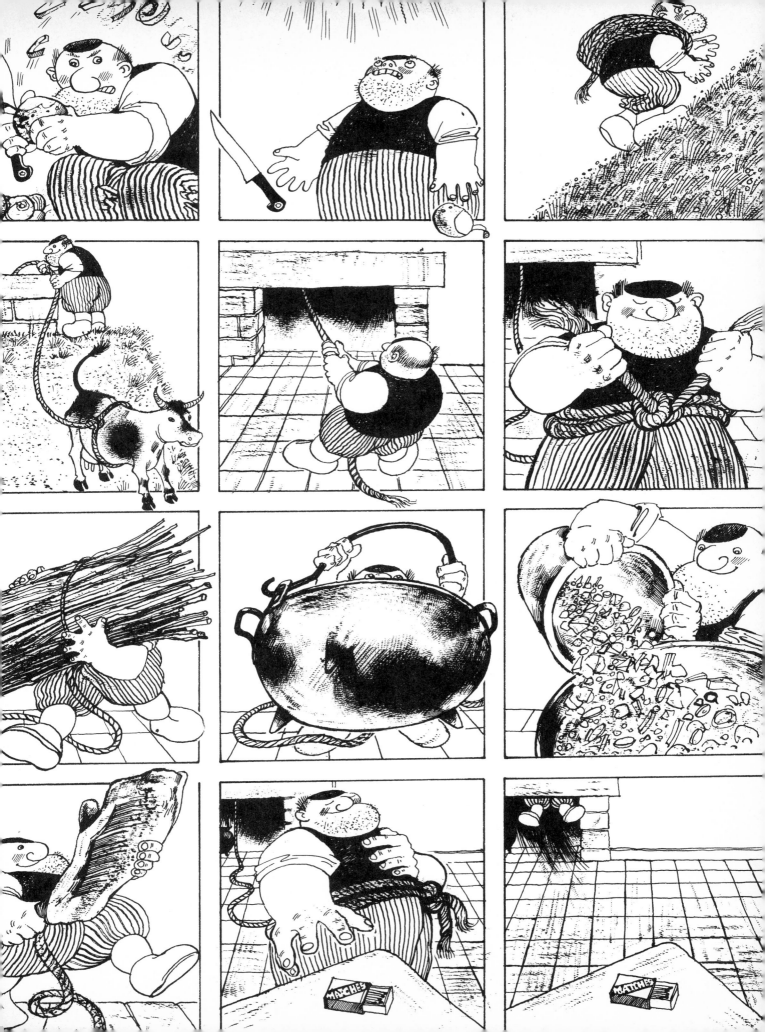

and Fritzl – well, he was whisked up into the chimney and there he dangled, poor man, and couldn't get up and couldn't get down.

Before long, there came Liesi home from the fields with the water jug in her hand and the scythe over her shoulder.

But Hulla. Hui. What was that dangling over the edge of the roof? The cow? Yes, the cow, and half-choked she was, too, with her eyes bulging and her tongue hanging out.

Liesi lost no time. She took her scythe – and ristch! rotsch! – the rope was cut and there was the cow wobbling on her four legs, but alive and well, heaven be praised!

Now Liesi saw the garden with its gate wide open. There were the pigs and goats and all the geese too. They were full to bursting, but the garden, alas! was empty.

Liesi walked on, and now what did she see? The churn upturned and Kinndli there in the sun, stiff and sticky with dried cream and butter.

Liesi looked at the cellar. There was the cider all over the floor and halfway up the stairs besides.

Liesi looked in the kitchen. The floor! It was piled high with peelings and parings, and littered with dishes and pans.

At last Liesi saw the fireplace. Hu! Hulla! Hui! What was that in the soup-kettle? Two arms were waving, two legs were kicking, and a gurgle, bubbly and weak-like was coming up out of the water.

"Na, na! What can this mean?" cried Liesi. She did not know (but we do – yes?) that when she saved the cow outside, something happened to Fritzl inside. Yes, yes, as soon as the cow's rope was cut, Fritzl, poor man, he dropped down the chimney and crash! splash! fell right into the kettle of soup in the fireplace.

Liesi lost no time. She pulled at the two arms and

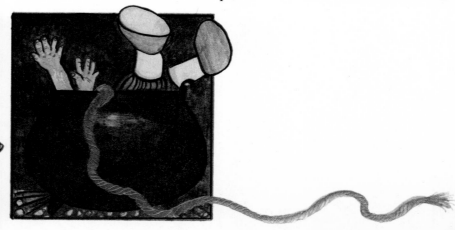

tugged at the two legs – and there, dripping and spluttering, with a cabbage-leaf in his hair, celery in his pocket, and a sprig of parsley over one ear, was her Fritzl.

"Na, na, my man!" said Liesi. "Is that the way you keep house – yes?"

"Oh Liesi, Liesi!" spluttered Fritzl. "You're right – that work of yours, 'tis none too easy."

"'Tis a little hard at first," said Liesi, "but tomorrow, maybe, you'll do better."

"Nay, nay!" cried Fritzl. "What's gone is gone, and so is my housework from this day on. Please, please, my Liesi – let me go back to my work in the fields, and never more will I say that my work is harder than yours."

"Well then," said Liesi, "if that's how it is, we surely can live in peace and happiness for ever and ever."

And that they did.

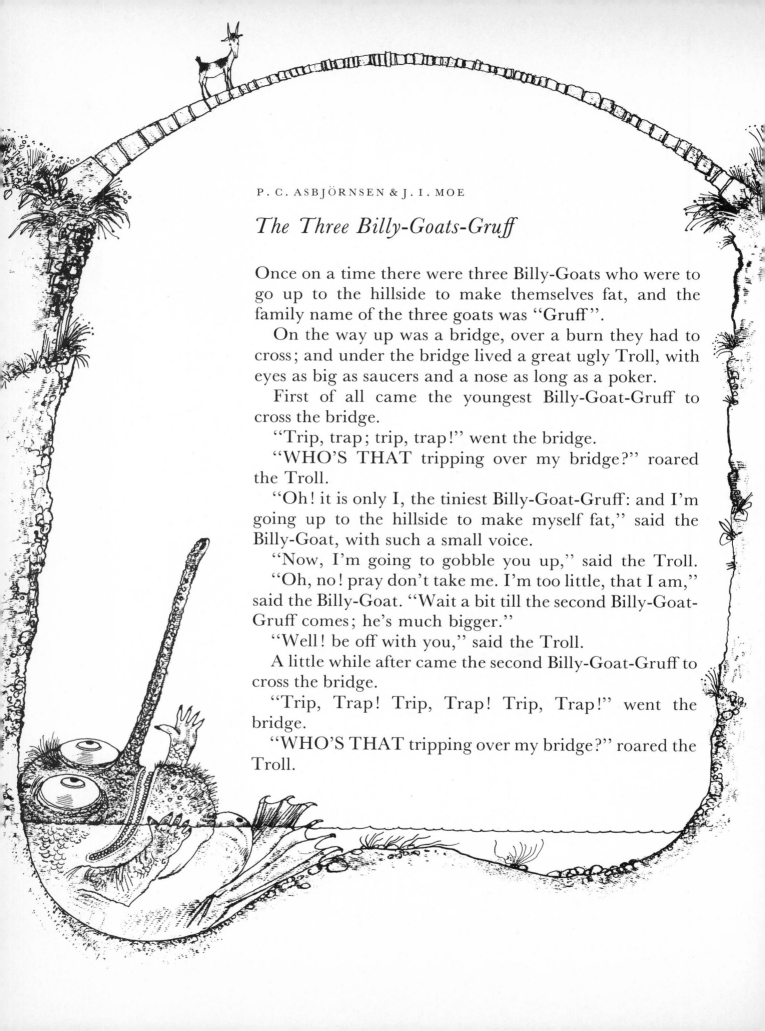

P. C. ASBJÖRNSEN & J. I. MOE

The Three Billy-Goats-Gruff

Once on a time there were three Billy-Goats who were to go up to the hillside to make themselves fat, and the family name of the three goats was "Gruff".

On the way up was a bridge, over a burn they had to cross; and under the bridge lived a great ugly Troll, with eyes as big as saucers and a nose as long as a poker.

First of all came the youngest Billy-Goat-Gruff to cross the bridge.

"Trip, trap; trip, trap!" went the bridge.

"WHO'S THAT tripping over my bridge?" roared the Troll.

"Oh! it is only I, the tiniest Billy-Goat-Gruff: and I'm going up to the hillside to make myself fat," said the Billy-Goat, with such a small voice.

"Now, I'm going to gobble you up," said the Troll.

"Oh, no! pray don't take me. I'm too little, that I am," said the Billy-Goat. "Wait a bit till the second Billy-Goat-Gruff comes; he's much bigger."

"Well! be off with you," said the Troll.

A little while after came the second Billy-Goat-Gruff to cross the bridge.

"Trip, Trap! Trip, Trap! Trip, Trap!" went the bridge.

"WHO'S THAT tripping over my bridge?" roared the Troll.

"Oh! it's the second Billy-Goat-Gruff, and I'm going up to the hillside to make myself fat," said the Billy-Goat, who hadn't such a small voice.

"Now, I'm going to gobble you up," said the Troll.

"Oh, no! don't take me. Wait a little till the big Billy-Goat-Gruff comes: he's much bigger."

"Very well; be off with you," said the Troll.

But just then up came the big Billy-Goat-Gruff.

"*Trip, Trap! Trip, Trap! Trip, Trap!*" went the bridge, for the Billy-Goat was so heavy that the bridge creaked and groaned under him.

"WHO'S THAT tramping over my bridge?" roared the Troll.

"It's I! THE BIG BILLY-GOAT-GRUFF," said the Billy-Goat, who had a big hoarse voice of his own.

"Now, I'm coming to gobble you up," roared the Troll.

"Well, come along! I've got two spears,
And I'll poke your eyeballs out at your ears,
I've got besides two curling-stones,
And I'll crush you to bits, body and bones."

That was what the big Billy-Goat said: so he flew at the Troll and poked his eyes out with his horns, and crushed him to bits, body and bones, and tossed him out into the burn, and after that he went up to the hillside. There the Billy-Goats got so fat they were scarcely able to walk home again; and if the fat hasn't fallen off them, why they're still fat; and so –

Snip, snap, snout,
This tale's told out.

The Golden Goose

There was a man who had three sons, the youngest of whom was called the Simpleton, and was despised, laughed at, and neglected, on every occasion. It happened one day that the eldest son wished to go into the forest to cut wood, and before he went his mother gave him a delicious pancake and a flask of wine, that he might not suffer from hunger or thirst. When he came into the forest a little old grey man met him, who wished him good day, and said,

"Give me a bit of cake out of your pocket, and let me have a drink of your wine; I am so hungry and thirsty."

But the prudent youth answered,

"Give you my cake and my wine? I haven't got any: be off with you."

And leaving the little man standing there, he went off. Then he began to fell a tree, but he had not been at it long before he made a wrong stroke, and the hatchet hit him in the arm, so that he was obliged to go home and get it bound up. That was what came of the little grey man.

Afterwards the second son went into the wood, and the mother gave to him, as to the eldest, a pancake and a flask of wine. The little old grey man met him also, and begged for a little bit of cake and a drink of wine. But the second son spoke out plainly, saying,

"What I give you I lose myself, so be off with you."

And leaving the little man standing there, he went off. The punishment followed; as he was chopping away at the tree, he hit himself in the leg so severely that he had to be carried home.

Then said the Simpleton,

"Father, let me go for once into the forest to cut wood," and the father answered, "Your brothers have hurt themselves by so doing: give it up, you understand nothing about it."

But the Simpleton went on begging so long that the father said at last,

"Well, be off with you; you will only learn by experience."

The mother gave him a cake (it was only made with water, and baked in the ashes), and with it a flask of sour beer. When he came into the forest the little old grey man met him, and greeted him, saying,

"Give me a bit of your cake, and a drink from your flask; I am so hungry and thirsty."

And the Simpleton answered, "I have only a flour and water cake and sour beer; but if that is good enough for you, let us sit down together and eat." Then they sat down, and as the Simpleton took out his flour and water cake it became a rich pancake, and his sour beer became good wine; then they ate and drank, and afterwards the little man said,

"As you have such a kind heart, and share what you have so willingly, I will bestow good luck upon you. Yonder stands an old tree; cut it down, and at its roots you will find something," and thereupon the little man took his departure.

The Simpleton went there, and hewed away at the tree, and when it fell he saw, sitting among the roots, a goose with feathers of pure gold. He lifted it out and took

it with him to an inn where he intended to stay the night.
The landlord had three daughters who, when they saw
the goose, were curious to know what wonderful kind of
bird it was, and ended by longing for one·of its golden
feathers. The eldest thought, "I will wait for a good
opportunity, and then I will pull out one of its feathers for
myself," and so, when the Simpleton was gone out, she
seized the goose by its wing – but there her finger and hand
had to stay, held fast. Soon after came the second sister
with the same idea of plucking out one of the golden
feathers for herself; but scarcely had she touched her
sister, than she also was obliged to stay, held fast. Lastly
came the third with the same intentions; but the others
screamed out,

"Stay away! for heaven's sake stay away!"

But she did not see why she should stay away, and
thought, "If they do so, why should not I?" and went
towards them. But when she reached her sisters there she
stopped, hanging on with them. And so they had to stay,
all night. The next morning the Simpleton took the goose
under his arm and went away, unmindful of the three
girls that hung on to it. The three had always to run after
him, left and right, wherever his legs carried him. In the
midst of the fields they met the parson, who, when he saw
the procession, said,

"Shame on you, girls, running after a young fellow
through the fields like this," and forthwith he seized hold
of the youngest by the hand to drag her away, but hardly
had he touched her when he too was obliged to run after
them himself. Not long after the sexton came that way,
and seeing the respected parson following at the heels of the
three girls, he called out,

"Ho, your reverence, whither away so quickly? You
forget that we have another christening today;" and he

seized hold of him by his gown; but no sooner had he touched him than he was obliged to follow on too. As the five tramped on, one after another, two peasants with their hoes came up from the fields, and the parson cried out to them, and begged them to come and set him and the sexton free, but no sooner had they touched the sexton than they had to follow on too: and now there were seven following the Simpleton and the goose.

By and by they came to a town where a king reigned, who had an only daughter who was so serious that no one could make her laugh; therefore the king had given out that whoever should make her laugh should have her in marriage. The Simpleton, when he heard this, went with his goose and his hangers-on into the presence of the king's daughter, and as soon as she saw the seven people following always one after the other, she burst out laughing, and seemed as if she could never stop. And so the Simpleton earned a right to her as his bride: but the king did not like him for a son-in-law and made all kinds of objections, and said he must first bring a man who could drink up a whole cellar of wine. The Simpleton thought that the little grey man would be able to help him, and went out into the forest, and there, on the very spot where he felled the tree, he saw a man sitting with a very sad countenance. The Simpleton asked him what was the matter, and he answered,

"I have a great thirst, which I cannot quench: cold water does not agree with me: I have indeed drunk up a whole cask of wine, but what good is a drop like that?"

Then said the Simpleton,

"I can help you: only come with me, and you shall have enough."

He took him straight to the king's cellar, and the man sat himself down before the big vats, and drank, and

drank, and before a day was over he had drunk up the whole cellarfull. The Simpleton again asked for his bride, but the king was annoyed that a wretched fellow, called the Simpleton by everybody, should carry off his daughter, and so he made new conditions. He was to produce a man who could eat up a mountain of bread. The Simpleton did not hesitate long, but ran quickly off to the forest, and there in the same place sat a man who had fastened a strap round his body, making a very piteous face, and saying,

"I have eaten a whole bakehouse full of rolls, but what is the use of that when one is so hungry as I am? My stomach feels quite empty, and I am obliged to strap myself together, that I may not die of hunger."

The Simpleton was quite glad of this, and said,

"Get up quickly, and come along with me, and you shall have enough to eat."

He led him straight to the king's courtyard, where all the meal in the kingdom had been collected and baked into a mountain of bread. The man out of the forest settled himself down before it and hastened to eat, and in one day the whole mountain had disappeared.

Then the Simpleton asked for his bride the third time. The king, however, found one more excuse, and said he must have a ship that should be able to sail on land or on water.

"So soon," said he, "as you come sailing along with it, you shall have my daughter for your wife."

The Simpleton went straight to the forest, and there sat the little old grey man with whom he had shared his cake, and he said,

"I have eaten for you, and I have drunk for you, I will also give you the ship: and all because you were kind to me at the first."

Then he gave him the ship that could sail on land and on water, and when the king saw it he knew he could no longer withhold his daughter. The marriage took place immediately, and at the death of the king the Simpleton possessed the kingdom, and lived long and happily with his wife.

ANDREW LANG

The Half-Chick

Once upon a time there was a handsome black Spanish hen who had a large brood of chickens. They were all fine, plump little birds except the youngest, who was quite unlike his brothers and sisters. Indeed, he was such a strange, queer-looking creature that when he first chipped his shell his mother could scarcely believe her eyes, he was so different from the twelve other fluffy, downy, soft little chicks who nestled under her wings. This one looked just as if he had been cut in two. He had only one leg, and one wing, and one eye, and he had half a head and half a beak. His mother shook her head sadly as she looked at him and said:

"My youngest born is only a half-chick. He can never grow up a tall handsome cock like his brothers. They will go out into the world and rule over poultry yards of their own; but this poor little fellow will always have to stay at home with his mother." And she called him Medio Pollito, which is Spanish for half-chick.

Now, though Medio Pollito was such an odd, helpless-looking little thing, his mother soon found that he was not at all willing to remain under her wing and protection. Indeed, in character he was as unlike his brothers and sisters as he was in appearance. They were good, obedient chickens, and when the old hen clucked after them they chirped and ran back to her side. But Medio Pollito had a

roving spirit in spite of his one leg, and when his mother called to him to return to the coop, he pretended that he could not hear, because he had only one ear.

When she took the whole family out for a walk in the fields, Medio Pollito would hop away by himself and hide among the corn. Many an anxious minute his brothers and sisters had looking for him, while his mother ran to and fro cackling in fear and dismay.

As he grew older he became more self-willed and disobedient, and his manner to his mother was often very rude and his temper to the other chickens very disagreeable.

One day he had been out for a longer expedition than usual in the fields. On his return he strutted up to his mother with the peculiar little hop and kick which was his way of walking, and cocking his one eye at her in a very bold way he said:

"Mother, I am tired of this life in a dull farmyard, with nothing but a dreary maize field to look at. I'm off to Madrid to see the king."

"To Madrid, Medio Pollito!" exclaimed his mother. "Why, you silly chick, it would be a long journey for a grown-up cock, and a poor little thing like you would be tired out before you had gone half the distance. No, no, stay at home with your mother, and some day, when you are bigger, we will go a little journey together."

But Medio Pollito had made up his mind, and he would not listen to his mother's advice nor to the prayers and entreaties of his brothers and sisters.

"What is the use of our all crowding each other up in this poky little place?" he said. "When I have a fine courtyard of my own at the king's palace, I shall perhaps ask some of you to come and pay me a short visit."

And scarcely waiting to say goodbye to his family,

67

away he stumped down the high road that led to Madrid.

"Be sure that you are kind and civil to everyone you meet," called his mother, running after him; but he was in such a hurry to be off that he did not wait to answer her or even to look back.

A little later in the day, as he was taking a short cut through a field, he passed a stream. Now, the stream was all choked up and overgrown with weeds and water plants, so that its waters could not flow freely.

"Oh! Medio Pollito," it cried as the half-chick hopped along its banks, "do come and help me by clearing away these weeds."

"Help you, indeed!" exclaimed Medio Pollito, tossing his head and shaking the few feathers in his tail. "Do you think I have nothing to do but to waste my time on such trifles? Help yourself and don't trouble busy travellers. I am off to Madrid to see the king," and hoppity-kick, hoppity-kick, away stumped Medio Pollito.

A little later he came to a fire that had been left by some gypsies in a wood. It was burning very low and would soon be out.

"Oh! Medio Pollito," cried the fire in a weak, wavering voice as the half-chick approached, "in a few minutes I shall go quite out unless you put some sticks and dry leaves upon me. Do help me or I shall die!"

"Help you, indeed," answered Medio Pollito. "I have other things to do. Gather sticks for yourself and don't trouble me. I am off to Madrid to see the king," and hoppity-kick, hoppity-kick, away stumped Medio Pollito.

The next morning, as he was getting near Madrid, he passed a large chestnut tree, in whose branches the wind was caught and entangled.

"Oh! Medio Pollito," called the wind, "do hop up here

and help me to get free of these branches. I cannot come away and it is so uncomfortable."

"It is your own fault for going there," answered Medio Pollito. "I can't waste all my morning stopping here to help you. Just shake yourself off, and don't hinder me, for I am off to Madrid to see the king," and hoppity-kick, hoppity-kick, away stumped Medio Pollito in great glee, for the towers and roofs of Madrid were now in sight. When he entered the town he saw before him a great splendid house, with soldiers standing before the gates. This he knew must be the king's palace, and he determined to hop up to the front gate and wait there until the king came out. But as he was hopping past one of the back windows the king's cook saw him.

"Here is the very thing I want," he exclaimed, "for the king has just sent a message to say that he must have chicken broth for his dinner." Opening the window he stretched out his arm, caught Medio Pollito, and popped him into the broth pot that was standing near the fire. Oh! How wet and clammy the water felt as it went over Medio Pollito's head, making his feathers cling to him.

"Water! Water!" he cried in his despair, "do have pity upon me and do not wet me like this."

"Ah! Medio Pollito," replied the water, "you would not help me when I was a little stream away on the fields. Now you must be punished."

Then the fire began to burn and scald Medio Pollito, and he danced and hopped from one side of the pot to the other, trying to get away from the heat and crying out in pain:

"Fire! Fire! Do not scorch me like this; you can't think how it hurts."

"Ah! Medio Pollito," answered the fire, "you would not help me when I was dying away in the wood. You are

being punished."

At last, just when the pain was so great that Medio Pollito thought he must die, the cook lifted up the lid of the pot to see if the broth was ready for the king's dinner.

"Look here!" he cried in horror, "this chick is quite useless. It is burned to a cinder. I can't send it up to the royal table." And opening the window he threw Medio Pollito out into the street. But the wind caught him up and whirled him through the air so quickly that Medio Pollito could scarcely breathe, and his heart beat against his side till he thought it would break.

"Oh, wind!" at last he gasped out, "if you hurry me along like this you will kill me. Do let me rest a moment, or—"

But he was so breathless that he could not finish his sentence.

"Ah! Medio Pollito," replied the wind, "when I was caught in the branches of the chestnut tree you would not help me. Now you are punished." And he swirled Medio Pollito over the roofs of the houses till they reached the highest church in the town, and there he left him fastened to the top of the steeple.

And there stands Medio Pollito to this day. And if you go to Madrid and walk through the streets till you come to the highest church, you will see Medio Pollito perched on his one leg on the steeple, with his one wing drooping at his side, and gazing sadly out of his one eye over the town.

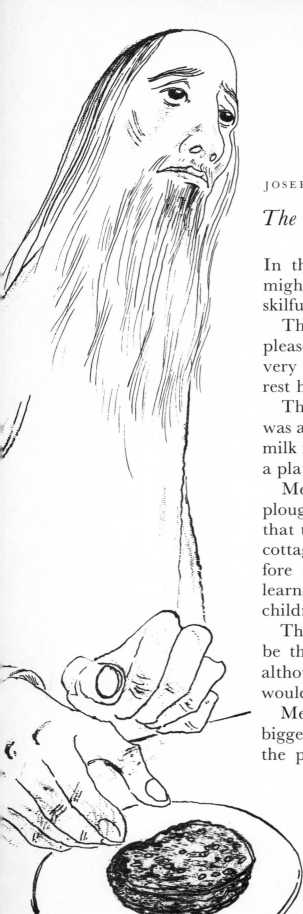

JOSEPH JACOBS

The History of Tom Thumb

In the days of the great Prince Arthur there lived a mighty magician, called Merlin, the most learned and skilful enchanter the world has ever seen.

This famous magician, who could take any form he pleased, was travelling about as a poor beggar, and being very tired he stopped at the cottage of a ploughman to rest himself, and asked for some food.

The countryman bade him welcome, and his wife, who was a very good-hearted woman, soon brought him some milk in a wooden bowl, and some coarse brown bread on a platter.

Merlin was much pleased with the kindness of the ploughman and his wife: but he could not help noticing that though everything was neat and comfortable in the cottage they both seemed to be very unhappy. He therefore asked them why they were so melancholy, and learned that they were miserable because they had no children.

The poor woman said, with tears in her eyes: "I should be the happiest creature in the world if I had a son; although he was no bigger than my husband's thumb, I would be satisfied."

Merlin was so much amused with the idea of a boy no bigger than a man's thumb that he determined to grant the poor woman's wish. Accordingly, in a short time

72

after, the ploughman's wife had a son, who, wonderful to relate! was not a bit bigger than his father's thumb.

The queen of the fairies, wishing to see the little fellow, came in at the window while the mother was sitting up in the bed admiring him. The queen kissed the child, and giving it the name of Tom Thumb, sent for some of the fairies, who dressed her little godson according to her orders:

> An oak-leaf hat he had for his crown:
> His shirt of web by spiders spun;
> His jacket wove of thistle's down:
> His trowsers were of feathers done.
> His stockings, of apple-rind, they tie
> With eyelash from his mother's eye:
> His shoes were made of mouse's skin,
> Tann'd with the downy hair within.

Tom never grew any larger than his father's thumb, which was only of ordinary size: but as he got older he became very cunning and full of tricks. When he was old enough to play with the boys, and had lost all his own cherry-stones, he used to creep into the bags of his play-fellows, fill his pockets, and, getting out without their noticing him, would again join in the game.

One day, however, as he was coming out of a bag of cherry-stones, where he had been stealing as usual, the boy to whom it belonged chanced to see him. "Ah, ah! my little Tommy," said the boy, "so I have caught you stealing my cherry-stones at last, and you shall be rewarded for your thievish tricks." On saying this, he drew the string tight round his neck, and gave the bag such a hearty shake that poor little Tom's legs, thighs, and body were sadly bruised. He roared out with pain, and begged to be let out, promising never to steal again.

A short time afterwards his mother was making a

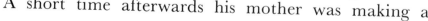

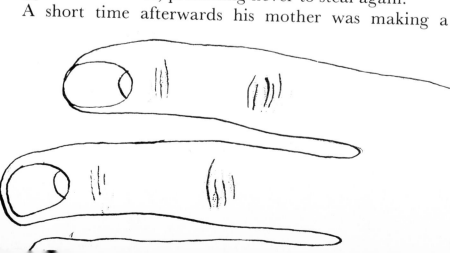

batter-pudding, and Tom, being very anxious to see how it was made, climbed up to the edge of the bowl: but his foot slipped, and he plumped over head and ears into the batter, without his mother noticing him, who stirred him into the pudding-bag, and put him in the pot to boil.

The batter filled Tom's mouth, and prevented him from crying; but on feeling the hot water, he kicked and struggled so much in the pot that his mother thought that the pudding was bewitched, and, pulling it out of the pot, she threw it outside the door. A poor tinker, who was passing by, lifted up the pudding, and, putting it into his budget, he then walked off. As Tom had now got his mouth cleared of the batter, he then began to cry aloud, which so frightened the tinker that he flung down the pudding and ran away. The pudding being broke to pieces by the fall, Tom crept out covered all over with the batter, and walked home. His mother, who was very sorry to see her darling in such a woeful state, put him into a teacup, and soon washed off the batter; after which she kissed him, and laid him in bed.

Soon after the adventure of the pudding, Tom's mother went to milk her cow in the meadow, and she took him along with her. As the wind was very high, for fear of his being blown away, she tied him to a thistle with a piece of fine thread. The cow soon observed Tom's oak-leaf hat, and liking the appearance of it, took poor Tom and the thistle at one mouthful. While the cow was chewing the thistle, Tom was afraid of her great teeth, which threatened to crush him in pieces, and he roared out as loud as he could: "Mother, Mother!"

"Where are you, Tommy, my dear Tommy?" said his mother.

"Here, mother," replied he, "in the red cow's mouth."

His mother began to cry and wring her hands; but the

cow, surprised at the odd noise in her throat, opened her mouth and let Tom out. Fortunately his mother caught him in her apron as he was falling to the ground, or he would have been dreadfully hurt. She then put Tom in her bosom and ran home with him.

Tom's father made him a whip of a barley straw to drive the cattle with, and having one day gone into the fields, Tom slipped a foot and rolled into the furrow. A raven, which was flying over, picked him up, and flew with him over the sea, and there dropped him.

A large fish swallowed Tom the moment he fell into the sea, which was soon after caught, and bought for the table of King Arthur. When they opened the fish in order to cook it, everyone was astonished at finding such a little boy, and Tom was quite delighted at being free again.

They carried him to the king, who made Tom his dwarf, and he soon grew a great favourite at court; for by his tricks and gambols he not only amused the king and queen, but also all the Knights of the Round Table.

It is said that when the king rode out on horseback, he often took Tom along with him, and if a shower came on, he used to creep into his majesty's waistcoat pocket, where he slept till the rain was over.

King Arthur one day asked Tom about his parents, wishing to know if they were as small as he was, and whether they were well off. Tom told the king that his father and mother were as tall as anybody about the court, but in rather poor circumstances. On hearing this, the king carried Tom to the treasury, the place where he kept all his money, and told him to take as much money as he could carry home to his parents, which made the poor little fellow caper with joy. Tom went immediately to procure a purse, which was made of a water-bubble, and then returned to the treasury, where he received a silver three-penny-piece to put into it.

Our little hero had some difficulty in lifting the burden upon his back; but he at last succeeded in getting it placed to his mind, and set forward on his journey. However, without meeting with any accident, and after resting himself more than a hundred times by the way, in two days and two nights he reached his father's house in safety. Tom had travelled forty-eight hours with a huge silver-piece on his back, and was almost tired to death, when his mother ran out to meet him, and carried him into the house. But he soon returned to court.

As Tom's clothes had suffered much in the batter-pudding, and the inside of the fish, his majesty ordered him a new suit of clothes, and to be mounted as a knight on a mouse.

Of Butterfly's wings his shirt was made,
His boots of chicken's hide;
And by a nimble fairy blade,
Well learned in the tailoring trade,
His clothing was supplied.
A needle dangled by his side;
A dapper mouse he used to ride,
Thus strutted Tom in stately pride!

It was certainly very diverting to see Tom in this dress and mounted on the mouse, as he rode out a-hunting with the king and nobility, who were all ready to expire with laughter at Tom and his fine prancing charger.

The king was so charmed with his address that he ordered a little chair to be made, in order that Tom might sit upon his table, and also a palace of gold, a span high, with a door an inch wide, to live in. He also gave him a coach, drawn by six small mice.

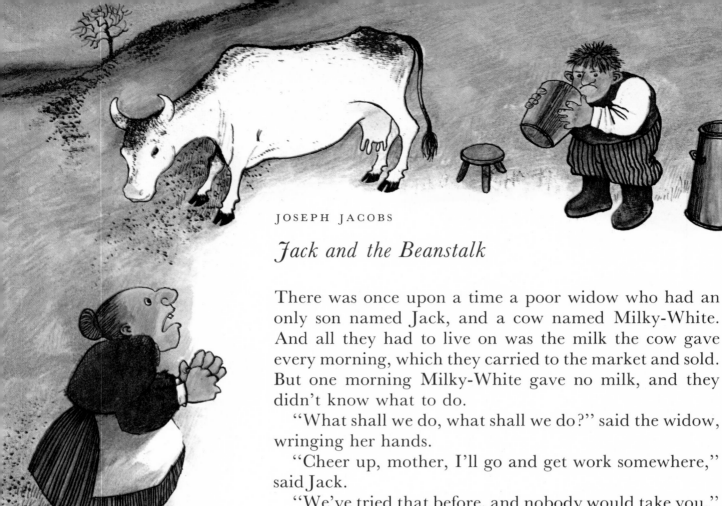

JOSEPH JACOBS

Jack and the Beanstalk

There was once upon a time a poor widow who had an only son named Jack, and a cow named Milky-White. And all they had to live on was the milk the cow gave every morning, which they carried to the market and sold. But one morning Milky-White gave no milk, and they didn't know what to do.

"What shall we do, what shall we do?" said the widow, wringing her hands.

"Cheer up, mother, I'll go and get work somewhere," said Jack.

"We've tried that before, and nobody would take you," said his mother; "we must sell Milky-White and with the money start shop, or something."

"All right, mother," says Jack, "it's market-day today, and I'll soon sell Milky-White, and then we'll see what we can do."

So he took the cow's halter in his hand, and off he started. He hadn't gone far when he met a funny-looking old man, who said to him: "Good morning, Jack."

"Good morning to you," said Jack, and wondered how he knew his name.

"Well, Jack, and where are you off to?" said the man.

"I'm going to market to sell our cow here."

"Oh, you look the proper sort of chap to sell cows," said the man; "I wonder if you know how many beans make five."

78

"Two in each hand and one in your mouth," says Jack, as sharp as a needle.

"Right you are," says the man, "and here they are the very beans themselves," he went on, pulling out of his pocket a number of strange-looking beans. "As you are so sharp," says he, "I don't mind doing a swop with you – your cow for these beans."

"Go along," says Jack; "wouldn't you like it?"

"Ah! you don't know what these beans are," said the man: "if you plant them overnight, by morning they grow right up to the sky."

"Really?" said Jack; "you don't say so."

"Yes, that is so, and if it doesn't turn out to be true you can have your cow back."

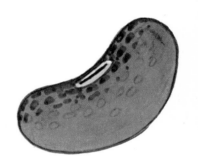

"Right," says Jack, and hands him over Milky-White's halter and pockets the beans.

Back goes Jack home, and as he hadn't gone very far it wasn't dusk by the time he got to his door.

"Back already, Jack?" said his mother; "I see you haven't got Milky-White, so you've sold her. How much did you get for her?"

"You'll never guess, mother," says Jack.

"No, you don't say so. Good boy! Five pounds, ten, fifteen, no, it can't be twenty."

"I told you you couldn't guess. What do you say to these beans: they're magical, plant them overnight and –"

"What!" says Jack's mother, "have you been such a fool, such a dolt, such an idiot, as to give away my Milky-White, the best milker in the parish, and prime beef to boot, for a set of paltry beans? Take that! Take that! Take that! And as for your precious beans here they go out of the window. And now off with you to bed. Not a sup shall you drink, and not a bite shall you swallow this very night."

79

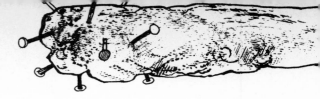

So Jack went upstairs to his little room in the attic, and sad and sorry he was, to be sure, as much for his mother's sake, as for the loss of his supper.

At last he dropped off to sleep.

When he woke up, the room looked so funny. The sun was shining into part of it, and yet all the rest was quite dark and shady. So Jack jumped up and dressed himself and went to the window. And what do you think he saw? Why, the beans his mother had thrown out of the window into the garden had sprung up into a big beanstalk which went up and up and up till it reached the sky. So the man spoke truth after all.

The beanstalk grew up quite close past Jack's window, so all he had to do was to open it and give a jump on to the beanstalk which ran up just like a big ladder. So Jack climbed, and he climbed and he climbed and he climbed and he climbed and he climbed till at last he reached the sky. And when he got there he found a long broad road going as straight as a dart. So he walked along and he walked along and he walked along till he came to a great big tall house, and on the doorstep there was a great big tall woman.

"Good morning, mum," says Jack, quite polite-like. "Could you be so kind as to give me some breakfast?" For he hadn't had anything to eat, you know, the night before and was as hungry as a hunter.

"It's breakfast you want, is it?" says the great big tall woman. "It's breakfast you'll be if you don't move off from here. My man is an ogre and there's nothing he likes better than boys broiled on toast. You'd better be moving on or he'll soon be coming."

"Oh! please, mum, do give me something to eat, mum. I've had nothing to eat since yesterday morning, really and truly, mum," says Jack. "I may as well be broiled as

die of hunger."

Well, the ogre's wife was not half so bad after all. So she took Jack into the kitchen, and gave him a hunk of bread and cheese and a jug of milk. But Jack hadn't half finished these when thump! thump! thump! the whole house began to tremble with the noise of someone coming.

"Goodness gracious me! It's my old man," said the ogre's wife, "what on earth shall I do? Come along quick and jump in here." And she bundled Jack into the oven just as the ogre came in.

He was a big one, to be sure. At his belt he had three calves strung up by the heels, and he unhooked them and threw them down on the table and said: "Here, wife, broil me a couple of these for breakfast. Ah! what's this I smell?

"Fee-fi-fo-fum,
I smell the blood of an Englishman,
Be he alive, or be he dead
I'll have his bones to grind my bread."

"Nonsense, dear," said his wife, "you're dreaming. Or perhaps you smell the scraps of that little boy you liked so much for yesterday's dinner. Here, you go and have a wash and tidy up, and by the time you come back your breakfast'll be ready for you."

So off the ogre went, and Jack was just going to jump out of the oven and run away when the woman told him not. "Wait till he's asleep," says she: "he always has a doze after breakfast."

Well, the ogre had his breakfast, and after that he goes to a big chest and takes out of it a couple of bags of gold, and down he sits and counts till at last his head began to nod and he began to snore till the whole house shook again.

81

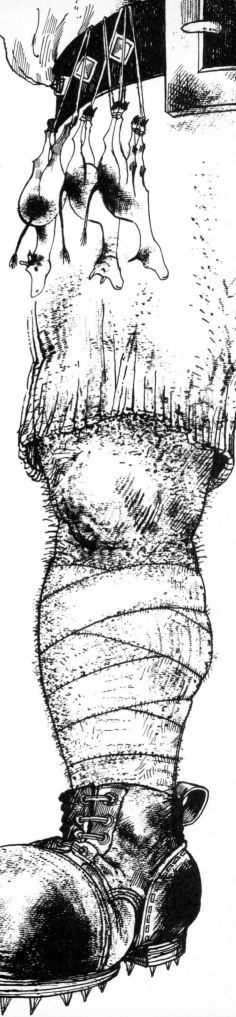

Then Jack crept out on tiptoe from his oven, and as he was passing the ogre he took one of the bags of gold under his arm, and off he pelters till he came to the beanstalk, and then he threw down the bag of gold, which, of course, fell into his mother's garden, and then he climbed down and climbed down till at last he got home and told his mother and showed her the gold and said: "Well, mother, wasn't I right about the beans? They are really magical, you see."

So they lived on the bag of gold for some time, but at last they came to the end of it, and Jack made up his mind to try his luck once more at the top of the beanstalk. So one fine morning he rose up early, and got on to the beanstalk, and he climbed and he climbed and he climbed and he climbed and he climbed and he climbed till at last he came out on to the road again and up to the great big tall house he had been to before. There, sure enough, was the great big tall woman a-standing on the doorstep.

"Good morning, mum," says Jack, as bold as brass, "could you be so good as to give me something to eat?"

"Go away, my boy," said the big tall woman, "or else my man will eat you up for breakfast. But aren't you the youngster who came here once before? Do you know, that very day my man missed one of his bags of gold."

"That's strange, mum," said Jack, "I dare say I could tell you something about that, but I'm so hungry I can't speak till I've had something to eat."

Well, the big tall woman was so curious that she took him in and gave him something to eat. But he had scarcely begun munching it as slowly as he could when thump! thump! they heard the giant's footstep, and his wife hid Jack away in the oven.

All happened as it did before. In came the ogre as he did before, said: "Fee-fi-fo-fum," and had his breakfast off

three broiled oxen. Then he said: "Wife, bring me the hen that lays the golden eggs." So she brought it, and the ogre said: "Lay," and it laid an egg all of gold. And then the ogre began to nod his head, and to snore till the house shook.

Then Jack crept out of the oven on tiptoe and caught hold of the golden hen, and was off before you could say "Jack Robinson". But this time the hen gave a cackle which woke the ogre, and just as Jack got out of the house he heard him calling, "Wife, wife, what have you done with my golden hen?"

And the wife said: "Why, my dear?"

But that was all Jack heard, for he rushed off to the beanstalk and climbed down like a house on fire. And when he got home he showed his mother the wonderful hen, and said "Lay" to it; and it laid a golden egg every time he said "Lay".

Well, Jack was not content, and it wasn't very long before he determined to have another try at his luck up there at the top of the beanstalk. So one fine morning, he rose up early, and got on to the beanstalk, and he climbed and he climbed and he climbed and he climbed till he got to the top. But this time he knew better than to go straight to the ogre's house. And when he got near it, he waited behind a bush till he saw the ogre's wife come out with a pail to get some water, and then he crept into the house and got into the copper. He hadn't been there long when he heard thump! thump! thump! as before, and in came the ogre and his wife.

"Fee-fi-fo-fum, I smell the blood of an Englishman," cried out the ogre. "I smell him, wife, I smell him."

"Do you, my dearie?" says the ogre's wife. "Then, if it's that little rogue that stole your gold and the hen that laid the golden egg he's sure to have got into the oven."

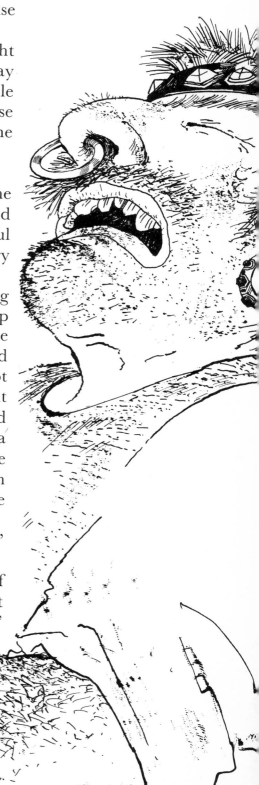

And they both rushed to the oven. But Jack wasn't there, luckily, and the ogre's wife said: "There you are again with your fee-fi-fo-fum. Why, of course, it's the boy you caught last night that I've just broiled for your breakfast. How forgetful I am, and how careless you are not to know the difference between live and dead after all these years."

So the ogre sat down to the breakfast and ate it, but every now and then he would mutter: "Well, I could have sworn –" and he'd get up and search the larder and the cupboards and everything, only, luckily, he didn't think of the copper.

After breakfast was over, the ogre called out: "Wife, wife, bring me my golden harp." So she brought it and put it on the table before him. Then he said: "Sing!" and the golden harp sang most beautifully. And it went on singing till the ogre fell asleep, and commenced to snore like thunder.

Then Jack lifted up the copper-lid very quietly and got down like a mouse and crept on hands and knees till he came to the table, when up he crawled, caught hold of the golden harp and dashed with it towards the door, but the harp called out quite loud: "Master! Master!" and the ogre woke up just in time to see Jack running off with his harp.

Jack ran as fast as he could, and the ogre came rushing after, and would soon have caught him only Jack had a start and dodged him a bit and knew where he was going. When he got to the beanstalk the ogre was not more than twenty yards away when suddenly he saw Jack disappear, and when he came to the end of the road he saw Jack underneath climbing down for dear life. Well, the ogre didn't like trusting himself to such a ladder, and he stood and waited, so Jack got another start. But just then the harp cried out: "Master! Master!" and the ogre swung

himself down on to the beanstalk, which shook with his weight. Down climbs Jack, and after him climbed the ogre. By this time Jack had climbed down and climbed down and climbed down till he was very nearly home. So he called out: "Mother! Mother! bring me an axe, bring me an axe." And his mother came rushing out with the axe in her hand, but when she came to the beanstalk she stood stock still with fright, for there she saw the ogre with his legs just through the clouds.

But Jack jumped down and got hold of the axe and gave a chop at the beanstalk which cut it half in two. The ogre felt the beanstalk shake and quiver, so he stopped to see what was the matter. Then Jack gave another chop with the axe, and the beanstalk was cut in two and began to topple over. Then the ogre fell down and broke his crown, and the beanstalk came toppling after.

Then Jack showed his mother his golden harp, and what with showing that and selling the golden eggs, Jack and his mother became very rich, and he married a great princess, and they lived happy ever after.

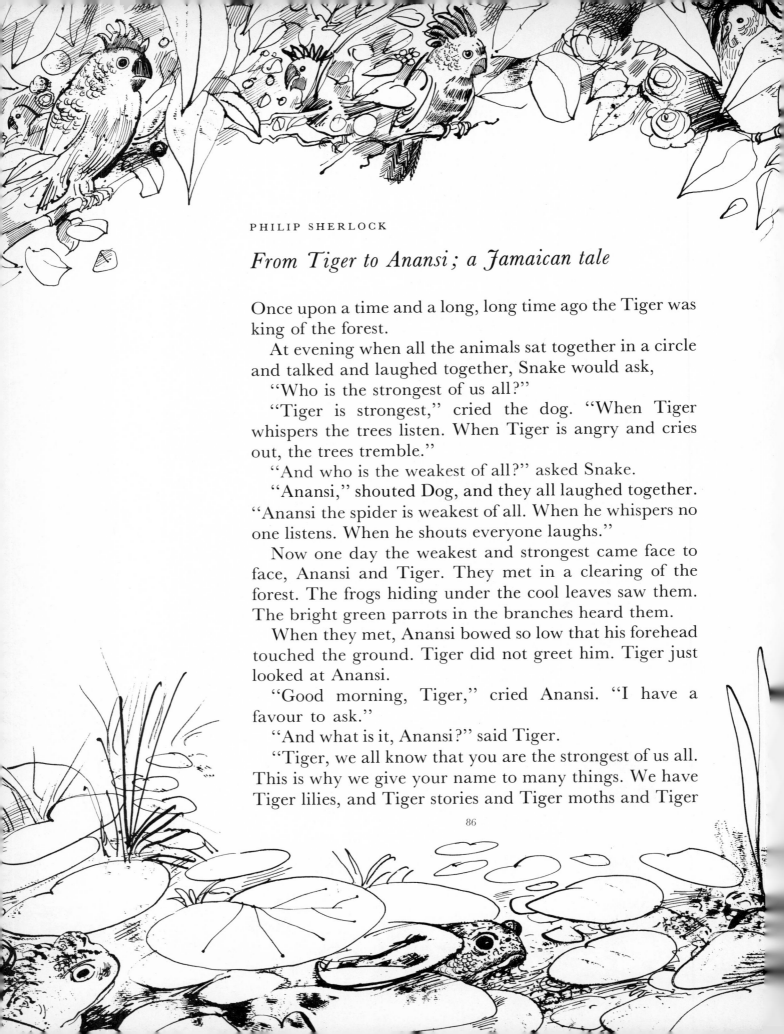

PHILIP SHERLOCK

From Tiger to Anansi; a Jamaican tale

Once upon a time and a long, long time ago the Tiger was king of the forest.

At evening when all the animals sat together in a circle and talked and laughed together, Snake would ask,

"Who is the strongest of us all?"

"Tiger is strongest," cried the dog. "When Tiger whispers the trees listen. When Tiger is angry and cries out, the trees tremble."

"And who is the weakest of all?" asked Snake.

"Anansi," shouted Dog, and they all laughed together. "Anansi the spider is weakest of all. When he whispers no one listens. When he shouts everyone laughs."

Now one day the weakest and strongest came face to face, Anansi and Tiger. They met in a clearing of the forest. The frogs hiding under the cool leaves saw them. The bright green parrots in the branches heard them.

When they met, Anansi bowed so low that his forehead touched the ground. Tiger did not greet him. Tiger just looked at Anansi.

"Good morning, Tiger," cried Anansi. "I have a favour to ask."

"And what is it, Anansi?" said Tiger.

"Tiger, we all know that you are the strongest of us all. This is why we give your name to many things. We have Tiger lilies, and Tiger stories and Tiger moths and Tiger

86

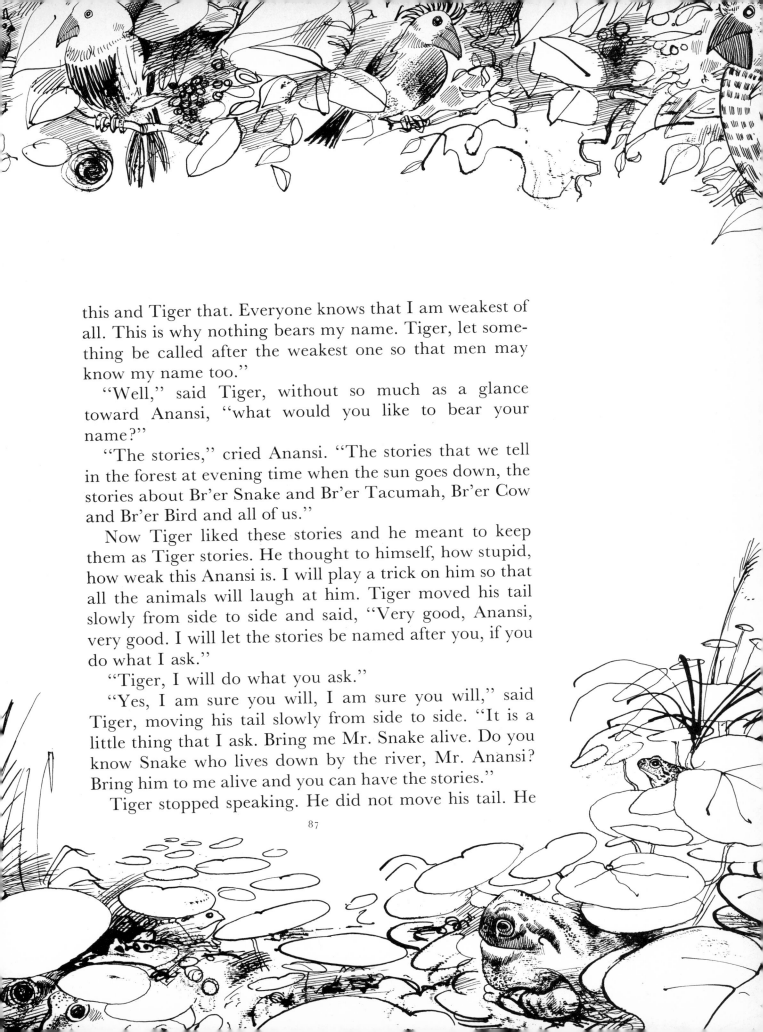

this and Tiger that. Everyone knows that I am weakest of all. This is why nothing bears my name. Tiger, let something be called after the weakest one so that men may know my name too."

"Well," said Tiger, without so much as a glance toward Anansi, "what would you like to bear your name?"

"The stories," cried Anansi. "The stories that we tell in the forest at evening time when the sun goes down, the stories about Br'er Snake and Br'er Tacumah, Br'er Cow and Br'er Bird and all of us."

Now Tiger liked these stories and he meant to keep them as Tiger stories. He thought to himself, how stupid, how weak this Anansi is. I will play a trick on him so that all the animals will laugh at him. Tiger moved his tail slowly from side to side and said, "Very good, Anansi, very good. I will let the stories be named after you, if you do what I ask."

"Tiger, I will do what you ask."

"Yes, I am sure you will, I am sure you will," said Tiger, moving his tail slowly from side to side. "It is a little thing that I ask. Bring me Mr. Snake alive. Do you know Snake who lives down by the river, Mr. Anansi? Bring him to me alive and you can have the stories."

Tiger stopped speaking. He did not move his tail. He

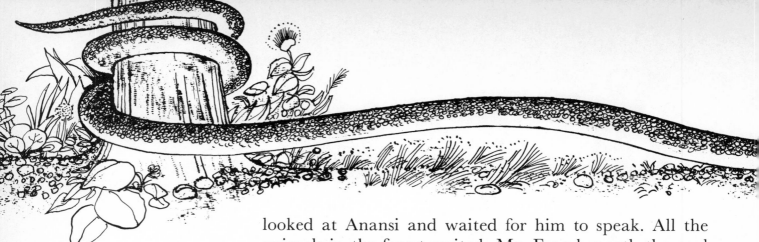

looked at Anansi and waited for him to speak. All the
animals in the forest waited. Mr. Frog beneath the cool
leaves, Mr. Parrot up in the tree, all watched Anansi.
They were all ready to laugh at him.

"Tiger, I will do what you ask," said Anansi. At these
words a great wave of laughter burst from the forest. The
frogs and parrots laughed. Tiger laughed loudest of all,
for how could feeble Anansi catch Snake alive?

Anansi went away. He heard the forest laughing at
him from every side.

That was on Monday morning. Anansi sat before his
house and thought of plan after plan. At last he hit upon
one that could not fail. He would build a Calaban.

On Tuesday morning Anansi built a Calaban. He
took a strong vine and made a noose. He hid the vine in
the grass. Inside the noose he set some of the berries that
Snake loved best. Then he waited. Soon Snake came up
the path. He saw the berries and went toward them. He
lay across the vine and ate the berries. Anansi pulled at
the vine to tighten the noose, but Snake's body was too
heavy. Anansi saw that the Calaban had failed.

Wednesday came. Anansi made a deep hole in the
ground. He made the sides slippery with grease. In the
bottom he put some of the bananas that Snake loved.
Then he hid in the bush beside the road and waited.

Snake came crawling down the path toward the river.
He was hungry and thirsty. He saw the bananas at the
bottom of the hole. He saw that the sides of the hole were

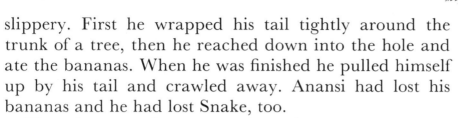

slippery. First he wrapped his tail tightly around the trunk of a tree, then he reached down into the hole and ate the bananas. When he was finished he pulled himself up by his tail and crawled away. Anansi had lost his bananas and he had lost Snake, too.

Thursday morning came. Anansi made a Fly Up. Inside the trap he put an egg. Snake came down the path. He was happy this morning, so happy that he lifted his head and a third of his long body from the ground. He just lowered his head, took up the egg in his mouth, and never even touched the trap. The Fly Up could not catch Snake.

What was Anansi to do? Friday morning came. He sat and thought all day. It was no use.

Now it was Saturday morning. This was the last day. Anansi went for a walk down by the river. He passed by the hole where Snake lived. There was Snake, his body hidden in the hole, his head resting on the ground at the entrance to the hole. It was early morning. Snake was watching the sun rise above the mountains.

"Good morning, Anansi," said Snake.

"Good morning, Snake," said Anansi.

"Anansi, I am very angry with you. You have been trying to catch me all week. You set a Fly Up to catch me. The day before you made a Slippery Hole for me. The day before that you made a Calaban. I have a good mind to kill you, Anansi."

"Ah, you are too clever, Snake," said Anansi. "You are

89

much too clever. Yes, what you say is so. I tried to catch you, but I failed. Now I can never prove that you are the longest animal in the world, longer even than the bamboo tree."

"Of course I am the longest of all animals," cried Snake. "I am much longer than the bamboo tree."

"What, longer than that bamboo tree across there?" asked Anansi.

"Of course I am," said Snake. "Look and see." Snake came out of the hole and stretched himself out at full length.

"Yes, you are very, very long," said Anansi, "but the bamboo tree is very long, too. Now that I look at you and at the bamboo tree I must say that the bamboo tree seems longer. But it's hard to say because it is farther away."

"Well, bring it nearer," cried Snake. "Cut it down and put it beside me. You will soon see that I am much longer."

Anansi ran to the bamboo tree and cut it down. He placed it on the ground and cut off all its branches. Bush, bush, bush, bush! There it was, long and straight as a flagstaff.

"Now put it beside me," said Snake.

Anansi put the long bamboo tree down on the ground beside Snake. Then he said:

"Snake, when I go up to see where your head is, you will crawl up. When I go down to see where your tail is, you will crawl down. In that way you will always seem to be longer than the bamboo tree, which really is longer than you are."

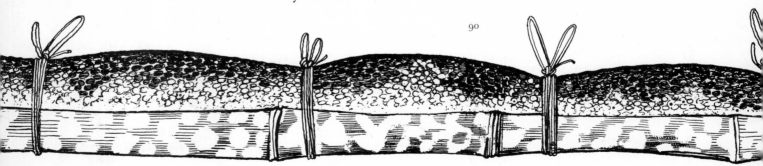

"Tie my tail, then!" said Snake. "Tie my tail! I know that I am longer than the bamboo, whatever you say."

Anansi tied Snake's tail to the end of the bamboo. Then he ran up to the other end.

"Stretch, Snake, stretch, and we will see who is longer."

A crowd of animals were gathering round. Here was something better than a race. "Stretch, Snake, stretch," they called.

Snake stretched as hard as he could. Anansi tied him around his middle so that he should not slip back. Now one more try. Snake knew that if he stretched hard enough he would prove to be longer than the bamboo.

Anansi ran up to him. "Rest yourself for a little, Snake, and then stretch again. If you can stretch another six inches you will be longer than the bamboo. Try your hardest. Stretch so that you even have to shut your eyes. Ready?"

"Yes," said Snake. Then Snake made a mighty effort. He stretched so hard that he had to squeeze his eyes shut. "Hooray!" cried the animals. "You are winning, Snake. Just two inches more."

And at that moment Anansi tied Snake's head to the bamboo. There he was. At last he had caught Snake, all by himself.

The animals fell silent. Yes, there Snake was, all tied up, ready to be taken to Tiger. And feeble Anansi had done this. They could laugh at him no more.

And never again did Tiger dare to call these stories by his name. They were Anansi stories forever after, from that day to this.

91

Budulinek

There was once a little boy named Budulinek. He lived with his old Granny in a cottage near a forest.

Granny went out to work every day. In the morning when she went away she always said:

"There, Budulinek, there's your dinner on the table and mind, you mustn't open the door no matter who knocks!"

One morning Granny said:

"Now, Budulinek, today I'm leaving you some soup for your dinner. Eat it when dinner time comes. And remember what I always say: don't open the door no matter who knocks."

She went away and pretty soon Lishka, the sly old mother fox, came and knocked on the door.

"Budulinek!" she called. "You know me! Open the door! Please!"

Budulinek called back:

"No, I mustn't open the door."

But Lishka, the sly old mother fox, kept on knocking.

"Listen, Budulinek," she said: "If you open the door, do you know what I'll do? I'll give you a ride on my tail!"

Now Budulinek thought to himself:

"Oh, that would be fun to ride on the tail of Lishka, the fox!"

So Budulinek forgot all about what Granny said to

92

him every day and opened the door.

Lishka, the sly old thing, came into the room and what do you think she did? Do you think she gave Budulinek a ride on her tail? Well, she didn't. She just went over to the table and gobbled up the bowl of soup that Granny had put there for Budulinek's dinner and then she ran away.

When dinner time came Budulinek hadn't anything to eat.

In the evening when Granny came home, she said:

"Budulinek, did you open the door and let any one in?"

Budulinek was crying because he was so hungry, and he said:

"Yes, I let in Lishka, the old mother fox, and she ate up all my dinner, too!"

Granny said: "Now, Budulinek, you see what happens when you open the door and let someone in. Another time remember what Granny says and don't open the door."

The next morning Granny cooked some porridge for Budulinek's dinner and said:

"Now, Budulinek, here's some porridge for your dinner. Remember: while I'm gone you must not open the door no matter who knocks."

Granny was no sooner out of sight than Lishka came again and knocked on the door.

"Oh, Budulinek!" she called. "Open the door and let me in!"

But Budulinek said: "No, I don't open the door!"

"Oh, now, Budulinek, please open the door!" Lishka begged. "You know me! Do you know what I'll do if you open the door? I'll give you a ride on my tail! Truly I will!"

Budulinek thought to himself:

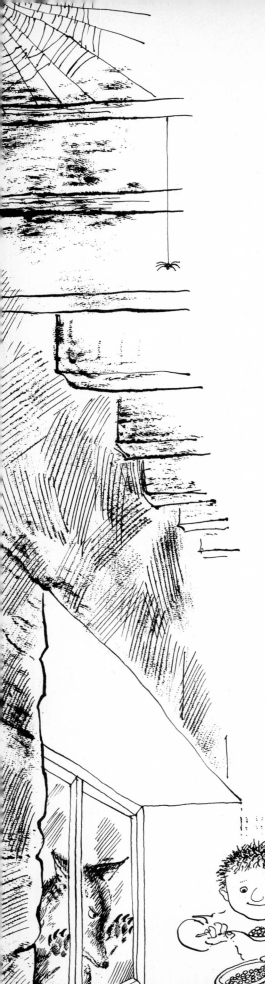

"This time maybe she will give me a ride on her tail."
So he opened the door.

Lishka came into the room, gobbled up Budulinek's porridge, and ran away without giving him any ride at all.

When dinner time came Budulinek hadn't anything to eat.

In the evening when Granny came home she said: "Budulinek, did you open the door and let any one in?"

Budulinek was crying again because he was so hungry, and he said:

"Yes, I let in Lishka, the old mother fox, and she ate up all my porridge, too."

"Budulinek, you're a bad boy!" Granny said. "If you open the door again, I'll have to spank you! Do you hear?"

The next morning before she went to work, Granny cooked some peas for Budulinek's dinner.

As soon as Granny was gone he began eating the peas, they were so good.

Presently Lishka, the fox, came and knocked on the door.

"Budulinek!" she called. "Open the door! I want to come in!"

But Budulinek wouldn't open the door. He took his bowl of peas and went to the window and ate them there where Lishka could see him.

"Oh, Budulinek!" Lishka begged. "You know me! Please open the door! This time I promise you I'll give you a ride on my tail! Truly I will!"

She just begged and begged until at last Budulinek opened the door. Then Lishka jumped into the room and do you know what she did? She put her nose right into the bowl of peas and gobbled them all up!

Then she said to Budulinek: "Now get on my tail and I'll give you a ride!"

94

So Budulinek climbed on Lishka's tail and Lishka went running around the room faster and faster until Budulinek was dizzy and just had to hold on with all his might.

Then, before Budulinek knew what was happening, Lishka slipped out of the house and ran swiftly off into the forest, home to her hole, with Budulinek still on her tail! She hid Budulinek down in her hole with her own three children and she wouldn't let him out. He had to stay there with the three little foxes and they all teased him and bit him. And then wasn't he sorry he had disobeyed his Granny! And, oh, how he cried!

When Granny came home she found the door open and no little Budulinek anywhere. She looked high and low, but no, there was no little Budulinek. She asked every one she met had they seen her little Budulinek, but nobody had. So poor Granny just cried and cried, she was so lonely and sad.

One day an organ-grinder with a wooden leg began playing in front of Granny's cottage. The music made her think of Budulinek.

"Organ-grinder," Granny said, "here's a penny for you. But, please, don't play any more. Your music makes me cry."

"Why does it make you cry?" the organ-grinder asked.

"Because it reminds me of Budulinek," Granny said, and she told the organ-grinder all about Budulinek and how somebody had stolen him away.

The organ-grinder said: "Poor Granny! I tell you what I'll do. As I go around and play my organ I'll keep my eyes open for Budulinek. If I find him I'll bring him back to you."

"Will you?" Granny cried. "If you bring me back my little Budulinek I'll give you a measure of rye and a measure of millet and a measure of poppy seed and a

measure of everything in the house!"

So the organ-grinder went off and everywhere he played his organ he looked for Budulinek. But he couldn't find him.

At last one day while he was walking through the forest he thought he heard a little boy crying. He looked around everywhere until he found a fox's hole.

"Oho!" he said to himself. "I believe that wicked old Lishka must have stolen Budulinek! She's probably keeping him here with her own three children! I'll soon find out."

So he put down his organ and began to play. And as he played he sang softly:

"One old fox,
And two, three, four,
And Budulinek
He makes one more!"

Old Lishka heard the music playing and she said to her oldest child: "Here, son, give the old man a penny and tell him to go away because my head aches."

So the oldest little fox climbed out of the hole and gave the organ-grinder a penny and said: "My mother says, please will you go away because her head aches."

As the organ-grinder reached over to take the penny, he caught the oldest little fox and stuffed him into a sack. Then he went on playing and singing:

"One old fox,
And two and three
And Budulinek
Makes four for me!"

Presently Lishka sent out her second child with a penny and the organ-grinder caught the second little fox in the same way and stuffed it also into the sack. Then he went on grinding his organ and softly singing:

"One old fox
And another for me,
And Budulinek
He makes the three."

"I wonder why that old man still plays his organ," Lishka said and sent out her third child with a penny.

So the organ-grinder caught the third little fox and stuffed it also into the sack. Then he kept on playing and singing softly:

"One old fox,
I'll soon get you!
And Budulinek
He makes just two."

And at last Lishka came out. So he caught her, too, and stuffed her in with her children. Then he sang:

"Four naughty foxes
Caught alive!
And Budulinek
He makes the five!"

The organ-grinder went to the hole and called down. "Budulinek! Budulinek! Come out!"

As there were no foxes left to hold him back, Budulinek was able to crawl out.

When he saw the organ-grinder he cried and said: "Oh, please, Mr. Organ-Grinder, I want to go home to my Granny!"

"I'll take you home to your Granny," the organ-grinder said, "but first I must punish these naughty foxes."

The organ-grinder cut a strong switch and gave the four foxes in the sack a terrible beating until they begged him to stop and promised that they would never again do anything to Budulinek.

Then the organ-grinder let them go and he took Budulinek home to Granny.

Granny was delighted to see her little Budulinek and she gave the organ-grinder a measure of rye and a measure of millet and a measure of poppy seed and a measure of everything else in the house.

And Budulinek never again opened the door!

The Sun and the Wind

The Sun and the Wind once had a quarrel as to which was the stronger. Each believed himself to be the more powerful. While they were arguing they saw a traveller walking along the country highway, wearing a great cloak.

"Here is a chance to test our strength," said the Wind; "let us see which of us is strong enough to make that traveller take off his cloak; the one who can do that shall be acknowledged the more powerful."

"Agreed," said the Sun.

Instantly the Wind began to blow; he puffed and tugged at the man's cloak, and raised a storm of hail and rain, to beat at it. But the colder it grew and the more it stormed, the tighter the traveller held his cloak around him. The Wind could not get it off.

Now it was the Sun's turn. He shone with all his beams on the man's shoulders. As it grew hotter and hotter, the man unfastened his cloak: then he threw it back; at last he took it off! The Sun had won.

100

AESOP (RETOLD BY JOSEPH JACOBS)

The Miller, his Son, and their Donkey

A miller, accompanied by his young son, was taking his donkey to market in hopes of finding a purchaser for him. On the road they met a troop of girls, laughing and talking, who exclaimed: "Did you ever see such a pair of fools? To be trudging along the dusty road when they might be riding!"

The Miller thought there was sense in what they said; so he made his son mount the donkey, and himself walked at the side.

Presently they met some of his old cronies, who greeted them and said, "You'll spoil that son of yours, letting him ride while you toil along on foot! Make him walk, young lazybones! It'll do him all the good in the world."

The Miller followed their advice, and took his son's place on the back of the donkey while the boy trudged along behind. They had not gone far when they overtook a party of women and children, and the Miller heard them say, "What a selfish old man! He himself rides in comfort, but lets his poor little boy follow as best he can on his own legs!" So he made his son get up behind him. Further along the road they met some travellers, who asked the Miller whether the donkey he was riding was his own property, or a beast hired for the occasion. He replied that it was his own, and that he was taking it to market to sell.

"Good heavens!" said they, "with a load like that the poor beast will be so exhausted by the time he gets there that no one will look at him. Why, you'd do better to carry him!"

"Anything to please you," said the old man, "we can but try." So they got off, tied the donkey's legs together with a rope and slung him on a pole, and at last reached the town, carrying him between them. This was so absurd a sight that the people ran out in crowds to laugh at it, and chaffed the father and son unmercifully, some even calling them lunatics. They had then got to a bridge over the river where the donkey, frightened by the noise and his unusual situation, kicked and struggled till he broke the ropes that bound him, and fell into the water and was drowned. Whereupon the unfortunate Miller, vexed and ashamed, made the best of his way home again, convinced that in trying to please all he had pleased none, and had lost his donkey in the bargain.

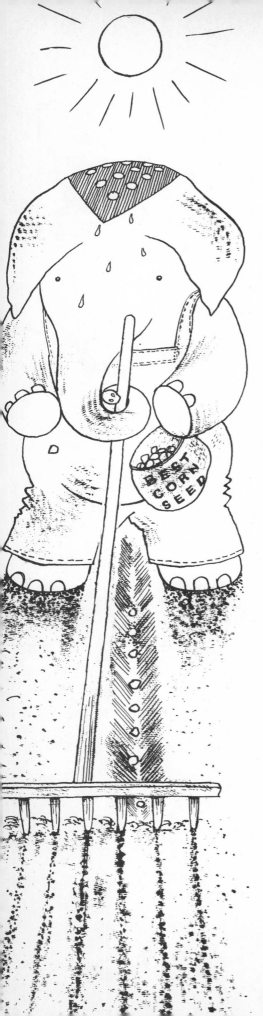

E. B. KALIBALA & MARY GOULD DAVIS

Wakaima and the Clay Man

Long, long ago there lived in Africa a rabbit who was called Wakaima. He was very lazy. His greatest friend was an elephant who was called Wanjovu. They lived together on a farm.

Now Wanjovu got tired of living with Wakaima, who was lazy and did not work at all while Wanjovu worked very hard. So one day he said:

"Let each have his own farm. You will have yours and I will have mine. Then we will share what we grow."

Wakaima agreed.

They each selected a plot of ground, prepared the soil and planted the seed. But instead of working on his farm Wakaima ran off into the jungle and spent the days eating wild fruit and sleeping under the trees. When evening came he would rub dirt over his paws and face and come into the house groaning, rubbing his back and saying how hard he had worked and how tired he was.

Wanjovu was a good gardener. He planted and cultivated corn and potatoes, peas and many other vegetables. When evening came he was really tired – but he said nothing about it.

Wakaima, coming in with a stick or two for the fire, his paws and face covered with dirt, would throw himself down before the fire. "How tired I am!" he would say. "The work has been so hard today. I have worked all day

without stopping."

Wanjovu, who really believed him, would prepare supper for them both. Then Wakaima would wash his paws and face and sit down to eat.

Now one evening as they sat down to the supper that Wanjovu had prepared, Wanjovu said:

"Wakaima, I am afraid that you work too hard on your farm."

Wakaima shook his head. "We cannot work too hard," he said. "We must have plenty of food to store away before the rains come."

This went on for weeks. Finally the crops were ready. The time had come to gather in the harvest.

One evening Wanjovu came in with a large basket filled with beautiful ears of corn and fine white potatoes. He cooked them very carefully, and he and Wakaima ate every one.

"How good the corn is, how sweet!" said Wakaima. "I have never eaten finer potatoes."

The next evening Wakaima came in with a basket full of corn and potatoes. "These are probably not as good as yours," he said. "But we will try them."

Wanjovu looked them over. They looked very much like the corn and potatoes from his own garden. He said nothing. He cooked them carefully, and they ate them for supper.

The next morning when Wanjovu went to his farm, he saw that someone had been there in the night and stolen some of his corn and some of his potatoes. That evening he said to Wakaima: "Someone got into my farm last night and stole some of my vegetables."

Wakaima pretended to be very much excited. "Some thief got into my farm, too," he said. "What are we going to do about it?"

105

Now Wakaima had stolen the things from Wanjovu himself. He had no vegetables in his garden.

"We must do something to keep the thief away," Wanjovu answered. "I will think it over and work out a plan."

The next day Wanjovu went to the river and got a large quantity of clay. With it he made a clay man, with arms outstretched. Carefully he carried the clay man to his farm and set it up between the corn and the potatoes. When he had finished it was quite dark.

Later the moon rose. There stood the clay man. There was his shadow, black in the white moonlight.

Wanjovu had been asleep in his own bed for hours when the little figure of Wakaima stole into his potato patch. When Wakaima saw the clay man looming up in the moonlight he was frightened. Could it be Wanjovu waiting to punish him for stealing the corn and the potatoes? He dared not move. The clay man did not move. Finally Wakaima gathered courage to speak: "Hullo, Wanjovu," he called. "What are you doing here at this time of night?"

The clay man did not answer.

Wakaima began to lose his temper.

"You are not Wanjovu!" he shouted. "You are a thief who has come to steal his corn. Answer me, or I will go at once and tell Wanjovu."

The clay man did not answer.

Wakaima drew nearer to him. He was puzzled. He said: "Who are you? Why do you not answer?"

The clay man did not answer.

Wakaima walked cautiously all around him. The clay man looked very large in the moonlight.

"If you do not answer me, I will hit you!" shouted Wakaima.

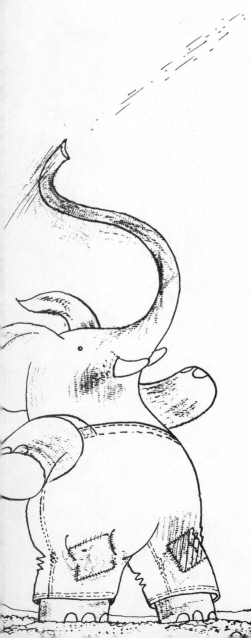

The clay man did not answer.

Wakaima went up to him and struck him as hard as he could with his paw. And his paw stuck to the soft clay.

"Let me go!" he screamed. "Let me go, or I will hit you with my other paw!"

But the clay man did not let him go.

Wakaima lifted his other paw and punched the clay man in the stomach as hard as he could.

And his other paw stuck in the soft clay. He was getting more angry every minute.

"Let me go, I tell you!" he shouted. "If you do not let me go, I will kick you with my foot."

But the clay man did not let him go.

Wakaima raised his foot and kicked the clay man. And his foot stuck in the soft clay. He tried his best to pull his foot away.

But the clay man would not let it go.

Wakaima was now very angry and very tired. He lifted his other foot and kicked the clay man with all his strength. And the other foot stuck in the soft clay.

"I will bite you with my teeth!" screamed Wakaima. "I will bite you in the stomach with my long, sharp teeth unless you let me go."

But the clay man did not let him go.

Wakaima butted his head against the clay man and set his long, sharp teeth into the clay. And the clay held him fast. He could not draw his teeth away. He could not draw his head away. His feet and his paws were held fast. He could not move. He could not call for help. He was held as if in a trap. The moon sank low in the sky. Darkness came. There was Wakaima, held by the clay man.

In the east the dawn broke slowly. Slowly the sun rose from its slumber behind the hills. The birds began to sing their morning songs. Very early Wanjovu got up and

went to his farm. He wanted to see if the clay man had trapped the thief. And he found Wakaima, held by the clay man.

"You wicked fellow!" he thundered. "So you are the thief who has stolen my food. Do you not have a farm of your own? I suppose it was easier to steal my corn and potatoes than to work over yours. What a lazy good-for-nothing you are! Now I shall punish you."

He pulled at Wakaima until he had freed him from the clay man. Poor Wakaima! He looked so ashamed and so wretched. Wanjovu could not help feeling a little sorry for him.

"What are you going to do with me?" sobbed Wakaima.

Wanjovu thought for a while. Finally he said: "I really ought to eat you. You have eaten my crops, so I should eat you. You did not tell the truth about your own garden."

"But you cannot eat me alive," protested Wakaima. "I will have to be dead before you eat me."

"Well, what do you want me to do?" Wanjovu asked uneasily. He did not feel very happy about eating his friend Wakaima.

Wakaima pointed to the jungle. "Throw me over there among the trees," he said. "Throw me very high among the branches. By the time I hit the ground, I will be dead. Then you can eat me."

Wanjovu lifted Wakaima. He threw him high up among the branches of the trees. But when Wakaima struck the ground he was not dead. He was not even hurt. He landed lightly on his feet and scampered away into the jungle. Wanjovu knew that he could not catch him. He went back to his farm.

Since that time Wanjovu and Wakaima have not spoken to one another.

THE BROTHERS GRIMM

The Bremen Town Musicians

Once upon a time a man had a donkey, which for many years had faithfully carried his grain to the mill. At last, however, the animal's strength began to fail and he was no longer of any use for work. His master then began to think about getting rid of him. The donkey felt there was something in the air, so he ran away – down the road to Bremen. There he thought he could become a town musician.

When he had gone a little way, he found a dog who lay panting on the road as though he had run himself off his legs.

"Well, why are you panting so, Growler?" asked the donkey.

"Ah," answered the dog, "just because I am old, and every day I get weaker. Also, because I can no longer keep up with the other dogs, my master wanted to kill me. So I ran away. But now, how am I to earn my bread?"

"Do you know what?" said the donkey. "I am going to Bremen. There I shall become a town musician. Come with me and take your part in the music. I shall play the lute, and you shall beat the kettledrum."

The dog agreed, and they went on.

A short time after, they came upon a cat, sitting in the road with a face as long as a wet week.

"Well, what has been bothering you, Whiskers?"

110

asked the donkey.

"Who can be cheerful when his neck is in danger?" said the cat. "I am getting old, and my teeth are dull. I prefer to sit by the stove and purr instead of hunting around after mice. Just because of this, my mistress wanted to drown me. I ran away, but now I don't know what is to become of me."

"Come with us to Bremen," said the donkey. "You are a great hand at serenading. You can become a town musician."

The cat agreed, and joined them.

Next, the three passed by a yard where a cock was sitting on the gate, crowing with all its might.

"Your crowing goes through and through one," said the donkey. "What's the matter?"

"Why – because Sunday visitors are coming tomorrow, the mistress ordered the cook to make me into soup! Now I am crowing with all my might while I have the chance."

"Come along, Redcomb," said the donkey. "We're going to Bremen. You'll find a much better life there. You have a strong voice. When we make music together, it will be good."

The cock agreed, and they all four went off together.

They could not, however, reach the town in one day. By evening they arrived at a wood, where they decided to spend the night.

The donkey and the dog lay down under a big tree. The cat and the cock settled themselves in the branches. The cock flew right up to the top, which was the safest place for him.

Before going to sleep, the cock looked around once more on every side. Suddenly he saw a light burning in the distance. He called out, "There must be a house not far off, for I see a light."

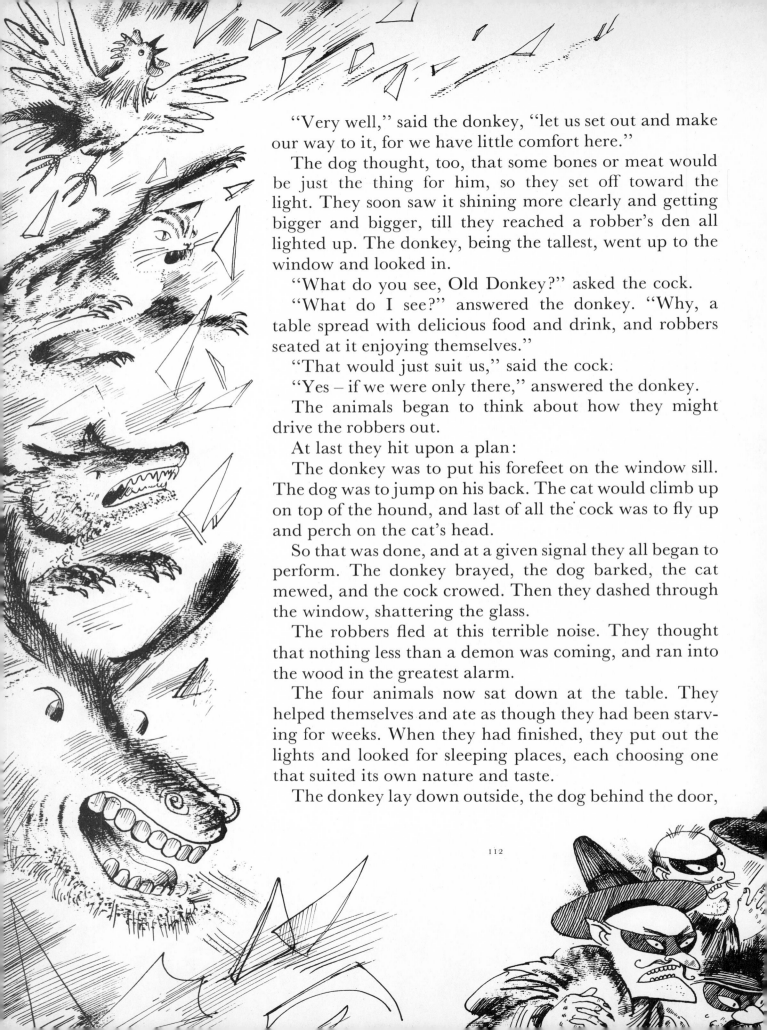

"Very well," said the donkey, "let us set out and make our way to it, for we have little comfort here."

The dog thought, too, that some bones or meat would be just the thing for him, so they set off toward the light. They soon saw it shining more clearly and getting bigger and bigger, till they reached a robber's den all lighted up. The donkey, being the tallest, went up to the window and looked in.

"What do you see, Old Donkey?" asked the cock.

"What do I see?" answered the donkey. "Why, a table spread with delicious food and drink, and robbers seated at it enjoying themselves."

"That would just suit us," said the cock:

"Yes – if we were only there," answered the donkey.

The animals began to think about how they might drive the robbers out.

At last they hit upon a plan:

The donkey was to put his forefeet on the window sill. The dog was to jump on his back. The cat would climb up on top of the hound, and last of all the cock was to fly up and perch on the cat's head.

So that was done, and at a given signal they all began to perform. The donkey brayed, the dog barked, the cat mewed, and the cock crowed. Then they dashed through the window, shattering the glass.

The robbers fled at this terrible noise. They thought that nothing less than a demon was coming, and ran into the wood in the greatest alarm.

The four animals now sat down at the table. They helped themselves and ate as though they had been starving for weeks. When they had finished, they put out the lights and looked for sleeping places, each choosing one that suited its own nature and taste.

The donkey lay down outside, the dog behind the door,

the cat on the hearth near the warm ashes, and the cock flew up to the rafters. As they were tired from their long journey, they soon went to sleep.

When midnight was past, and the robbers saw from a distance that the light was no longer burning and that all seemed quiet, the chief said, "We ought not to have been scared so easily."

He ordered one of the robbers to go back to examine the house.

The robber found everything quiet, and went on into the kitchen to kindle a light. Taking the cat's glowing, fiery eyes for live coals, he held a match close to them so as to light it. But the cat would stand no nonsense. It flew at his face, spitting and scratching. The man was terribly frightened and ran away.

He tried to get out by the back door, but the dog, who was lying there, jumped up and bit his leg. As the man ran on across the yard, the donkey gave him a good sound kick with his hind legs. The cock, who had been awakened by the noise and felt quite fresh and gay, cried out from his perch, "Cock-a-doodle-doo!"

Thereupon, the robber ran back as fast as he could to his chief, and said:

"There is a horrible witch in the house, who breathed on me and scratched me with her long fingers. Behind the door there stands a man with a knife, who stabbed me. In the yard lies a black monster, who hit me with a club. And upon the roof the judge is seated, and he called out 'Bring the rogue here!' So I ran away, as fast as I could."

From that time on, the robbers dared not go near that house, and the four Bremen musicians were so pleased with it that they never wished to leave it.

THE BROTHERS GRIMM

The Frog Prince

In the olden time, when wishing was some good, there lived a King whose daughters were all beautiful. But the youngest was loveliest of all. Even the sun, that looked on many things, marvelled when it shone upon her face.

Near the King's palace there was a large dark forest, and in the forest, under an old lime-tree, was a well. When the day was very hot the youngest Princess used to go into the forest and sit upon the edge of this cool well. When she was tired of doing nothing, she would play with a golden ball, throwing it up into the air and catching it again. This was her favourite game.

Now one day it happened that the ball did not fall back into her hand. It fell to the ground and rolled right into the well. The Princess followed it with her eyes as it sank in the water, but the well was so very deep that she could not see the bottom. Then she began to cry, louder and louder.

As she was crying, someone called out to her, "What is the matter, Princess? Your tears would move even a stone."

When she looked to the spot where the voice was coming from, she saw only a frog lifting its big ugly face out of the water.

"Oh, it's you, is it, old water-splasher? I am crying for my golden ball, which has fallen into the well."

"Be quiet then, and stop crying," answered the frog. "I know what to do. But what will you give me if I bring back your ball?"

"Whatever you like, you dear old frog," she said. "My clothes, my pearls and diamonds, or even the golden crown upon my head."

The frog answered, "I care not for your clothes, your pearls and diamonds, nor even your golden crown; but if you will let me be your playmate, and sit by you at table, and eat out of your plate, and drink out of your cup, and sleep upon your little bed – if you will promise to do all this, I will go down and fetch your ball."

"Oh, yes," she agreed quickly, "I promise all you ask, if only you will bring my ball back again to me."

To herself, the Princess thought, "What is the silly old frog chattering about? He lives in the well, croaking with his mates. He cannot live with a human being."

As soon as the frog had her promise, he ducked his head under the water and sank down. After a little while, back he came with the ball in his mouth, and threw it on the grass beside her.

The Princess was full of joy when she saw her pretty toy again. She picked it up, and ran off with it.

"Wait, wait!" cried the frog. "Take me with you. I can't run as fast as you can."

But what was the good of his crying *Croak, croak!* as loud as he could? The Princess did not listen to him. She ran home, and forgot all about the poor frog. He had to go back to his well again.

The next day, as the Princess was sitting at dinner with the King and all the court, eating from her golden plate, something came flopping up the stairs: *Flip, flap . . . Flip, flap.*

Soon there was a small rap on the door and a little voice

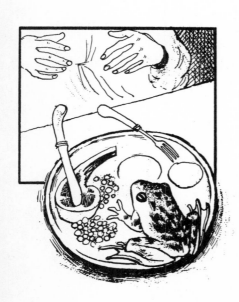

cried, "Youngest daughter of the King, you must let me in."

The Princess ran to see who it was. When she opened the door and saw the frog, she shut it again very quickly and went back to the table, for she was afraid.

The King noticed that her heart was beating very fast, and he said, "My child, what is the matter? Is there a giant at the door, wanting to take you away?"

"Oh, no!" she said. "It's not a giant, but a horrid frog."

"What does the frog want with you?"

"Oh, Father dear, last night when I was playing by the well in the forest, my golden ball fell into the water. And I cried, and the frog got it out for me. Then, because he insisted on it, I promised that he should be my playmate. I never thought that he would come out of his water, but there he is, and he wants to come in."

Then they heard the frog knock at the door a second time and cry:

"Youngest daughter of the King,
Open your door, I beg!
Remember your words of yesterday, and
Open your door, I beg!"

The King said, "What you have promised, you must do. Go and let the frog come in."

So she opened the door. The frog hopped in and followed her to her chair. There he sat, and cried, "Lift me up beside you." The Princess was slow about it, till at last the King ordered her to do it.

When the frog was put on the chair, he asked to be placed upon the table. Then he said, "Push your golden plate near me, that we may eat together." She did as he asked, but not happily.

The frog ate a good dinner, but the Princess could not eat a thing. At last he said, "I have eaten enough, and I

116

am tired. Carry me into your bedroom and arrange your bed, so that we may go to sleep."

The Princess began to cry, for she was afraid of the clammy frog, which she did not dare to touch, and which was now to sleep in her pretty little bed.

But the King grew very angry. He said, "What you have promised, you must now do."

So the Princess picked up the frog with her finger and thumb and carried him upstairs, where she put him in a corner of her room. When she had got into bed, he crept over and said, "I am tired, and I want to sleep as well as you do. Lift me up, or I will tell your father."

Then she became very angry. She picked him up and threw him with all her might against the wall, saying, "Now you may rest, you horrid frog!" But when he fell to the ground, he had changed from a frog into a handsome Prince with kind and beautiful eyes.

The Prince told her that a wicked fairy had turned him into a frog. Nobody could have freed him from the spell but the Princess herself.

Afterwards, at her father's wish, the Prince became the husband of the Princess.

When the sun rose on the day after the wedding, a coach drove up. It was drawn by eight milk-white horses, with white plumes on their heads and golden harness. Behind them stood faithful Henry, the Prince's servant, full of joy at his master's freedom. He had brought the coach to carry the young pair back to the Prince's own kingdom. The Prince and his bride rode away, and they lived happily ever after.

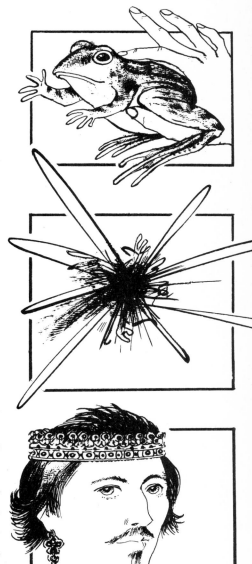

THE BROTHERS GRIMM

The Elves and the Shoemaker

There was once a shoemaker who, through no fault of his own, had become poor. Finally he had leather enough left to make only one more pair of shoes.

One night he cut out the shoes which he would sew the next morning. Then he lay down, said his prayers, and fell asleep.

In the morning, after he had said his prayers and was ready to sit down to work, he found a fine pair of shoes standing finished on his table. He was so astonished he did not know what to think!

He took the shoes in his hand to examine them closely. They were beautifully polished, and so neatly sewn that not one stitch was out of place. They were as good as the work of a master shoemaker.

Soon a customer came in. He was so pleased with the shoes that he paid much more than the usual price for them. Now the shoemaker had enough money to buy leather for two more pairs of shoes.

The shoemaker cut these out that evening. The next day, full of fresh courage, he was about to go to work. But he did not need to – for when he got to his table, he found the shoes finished!

Buyers were not lacking for these shoes, either. The shoemaker received so much money that he was able to buy leather for four pairs of shoes this time.

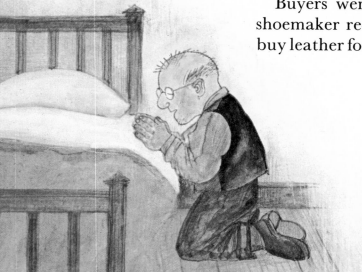

118

Early next morning he found the four pairs finished, beautifully; and so it went on. Whatever he cut out in the evening was finished by morning. The shoemaker was soon making a good living again, and became a well-to-do man.

One evening, not long before Christmas, when he had cut out some shoes as usual, the shoemaker said to his wife, "How would it be if we were to sit up tonight to see who it is that lends us such a good helping hand?"

The wife agreed, and lighted a candle. They hid themselves in the corner of the room, behind some clothes which were hanging there.

At midnight two little men came in through the window and sat down at the shoemaker's table. They took up the work lying cut out before them and began to stitch, sew, and hammer with their tiny fingers and tiny tools. They did this all so neatly and quickly that the shoemaker could not believe his eyes. The elves did not stop working till everything stood finished on the table. Then they ran quickly away.

The next day the wife said, "These little elves have made us rich. We are no longer hungry, and we ought to thank them. They run about with so little on – they must be freezing cold. I'll make them little shirts, coats, and trousers. I'll even knit each of them a cap and a pair of stockings, and you shall make them each a pair of shoes."

The husband agreed. By evening, they had all these presents ready. They laid on the table two tiny green suits, finely knit red stockings and caps, and shining pairs of little leather shoes. Then they hid themselves, to see how the elves would receive these.

At midnight the elves came skipping in, and were about to set to work. But, instead of finding leather ready, they found the beautiful little clothes.

At first they acted only surprised, but then greatly
delighted. As quickly as they could, they put on the little
shirts, coats, and trousers, the stockings and caps, and the
shoes. They smoothed them down and sang:

"Now we're boys so fine and neat,
Why cobble more for others' feet?"

They hopped and danced about, and leaped over the
chairs and tables. Then they ran away through the
window. From that time on, they were not seen again in
the shoemaker's shop. But the shoemaker did well as long
as he lived, and was lucky in everything he undertook.

CHARLES PERRAULT

Puss in Boots

Once a miller left to his three sons a mill, a donkey, and a cat.

The eldest took the mill and the second the donkey. The youngest had only the cat. The poor young fellow was quite unhappy at his lot.

"My brothers," said he, "may do well by joining together. But after I have eaten my cat and made a muff of his skin, I must die of hunger."

The cat, who heard all this, said to him: "Do not be sad, my good master. You need only give me a bag and have a pair of boots made for me so that I may scamper through the brambles. You shall see that you have not done so badly as you imagine."

The cat's master had often seen him play clever tricks to catch rats and mice. He would hang by his feet, or hide himself in the meal, and play dead. So the lad did not lose all hope of being helped.

When the cat received the boots, he pulled them on with a grand air. Then he put the bag about his neck, held its strings in his two forepaws, and went out to hunt for rabbits. He put bran and lettuce into his bag and stretched out beside it as if he were dead. He waited for young rabbits, who had not yet learned the tricks of the world, to crawl into the bag and eat what he had put there.

Scarcely had he lain down when he gained what he

wanted. A foolish young rabbit entered the bag. Puss, drawing close the strings, killed him without pity.

Proud of his catch, Puss carried it to the King's palace, and asked to speak with His Majesty.

He was shown into the King's rooms. Making a low bow, the cat said:

"I have brought you, sir, a rabbit, which my noble lord, the Marquis of Carabas" – that was the title Puss was pleased to give his master – "has commanded me to present to Your Majesty from him."

"Tell your master," said the King, "that I thank him, and that his present gives me a great deal of pleasure."

Another time the cat hid himself in a field of corn, holding his bag open. When a pair of partridges ran into it, he drew the strings and thus caught both of the birds. He gave them to the King as he had given him the rabbit. The King received the partridges happily, and ordered some money to be given to Puss.

The cat continued for two or three months to carry game to His Majesty. One day, when Puss knew that the King was to drive along the river with his daughter – who was the most beautiful Princess in the world – he said to his master, "If you will now follow my advice, your fortune is made. You have nothing to do but wash yourself in the river – I shall show you where – and leave the rest to me."

The Marquis of Carabas did what the cat advised, without knowing why. While he was bathing, the King passed by. The cat began to cry out as loudly as he could,

"Help! Help! My Lord Marquis of Carabas is drowning."

At this, the King put his head out of the coach window. He saw that it was the cat who had so often brought him such good game. He told his guards to run at once to the aid of the Marquis of Carabas.

FREE!
BEST BRAN
FRESH LETTUCE
Come in and
help yourself

While they were dragging the young man out of the river, the cat came up to the King's coach. He told the King that as his master was washing in the river, some robbers had run off with his clothes. The Marquis had cried, "Thieves! Thieves!" several times but no one had heard him. (Actually, the clever cat himself had hidden the clothes under a great stone.)

The King commanded his men to run and fetch one of his best suits for the Marquis of Carabas.

The fine clothes suited the Marquis, for he was well built and very handsome. The King's daughter took a secret liking for the Marquis. When he cast two or three respectful and tender glances upon her, she fell deeply in love with him.

The King invited the Marquis of Carabas to come into the coach and take the air with them. The cat, overjoyed to see his plan beginning to succeed, marched on ahead. Meeting some farm workers who were mowing a meadow, he said to them, "Good people, you who are mowing, if you do not tell the King that the meadow you are mowing belongs to My Lord Marquis of Carabas, you shall be chopped as fine as mincemeat."

The King did not fail to ask the mowers to whom the meadow belonged.

"To My Lord Marquis of Carabas," they answered. The cat's threat had made them terribly afraid.

"You have a fine place," said the King to the Marquis of Carabas.

"Yes," replied the Marquis, "this is a meadow which always gives a good harvest."

The cat, still running on ahead, now met some reapers. He said to them, "Good people, you who are reaping, if you do not tell the King that all this corn belongs to the Marquis of Carabas, you shall be chopped as fine as mincemeat."

The King, who passed by a moment after, wished to know to whom all that corn belonged.

"To My Lord Marquis of Carabas," replied the reapers.

The King was still more impressed.

The cat, going on ahead, said the same words to all he met. The King grew astonished at the vast lands held by the Marquis of Carabas.

Puss came at last to a stately castle. The master of this was an ogre, the richest ever known. He owned all the lands which the King had been riding through.

The cat had taken care to find out who this ogre was and what he could do. He asked to speak with him, saying smoothly that he could not pass so near his castle without paying his respects.

The ogre received him as politely as an ogre could, and made him sit down.

"I have been told," said the cat, "that you have the gift of being able to change yourself into any sort of creature. You can, for example, turn yourself into a lion or an elephant."

"That is true," answered the ogre roughly. "To prove it, I shall now become a lion."

Puss was so terrified at the sight of a lion so near him that he at once leaped out on the roof. And not without trouble and danger, because of his boots. These were of no use for walking upon the smooth tiles.

A little while later, when Puss saw that the ogre was no longer a lion, he came down and admitted he had been very much afraid.

"I have been told, also," said the cat, "but I cannot believe it, that you have the power to take on the shape of the smallest animal. For example, that you can change

125

yourself into a rat or even a mouse. I must say, I think this impossible."

"*Impossible*!" cried the ogre. "You shall see."

The ogre then changed himself into a mouse and began to run about the floor. Puss instantly fell on the mouse and ate him up.

Meanwhile the King, as he passed the ogre's fine castle, desired to go into it. Puss heard the noise of His Majesty's coach running over the drawbridge.

He ran out and said to the King, "Your Majesty is welcome to this castle of My Lord Marquis of Carabas."

"What, My Lord Marquis!" cried the King. "And does this castle, also, belong to you? There can be nothing finer than this court and all that surrounds it. Let us go in, if you please."

The Marquis gave his hand to the Princess and followed the King, who went first. They passed into a great hall, where they found a magnificent feast. This the ogre had prepared for his friends. They were that very day to visit him but now dared not enter, knowing the King was there.

His Majesty was as charmed with the Lord Marquis of Carabas as his daughter, who was so much in love with him.

The King said to the Marquis, "It is only for you to say, My Lord Marquis, whether you will be my son-in-law."

The Marquis, making several low bows, accepted the honour which His Majesty offered. That very day he married the Princess.

Puss became a great lord, and he never ran after mice any more – except for fun.

THE BROTHERS GRIMM

Snow-white

It was the middle of winter, and snow-flakes were falling like feathers from the sky. A queen sat at her window working, with an embroidery-frame of ebony. As she worked, gazing out on the snow, she pricked her finger, and there fell from it three drops of blood. When she saw how bright and red it looked, she said to herself, "Oh that I had a child as white as snow, as red as blood, and as black as the wood of the embroidery-frame!"

Not very long after this she had a daughter, with skin as white as snow, lips as red as blood, and hair as black as ebony, and she was named Snow-white. But when she was born the queen died.

After a year had gone by the king took another wife, a beautiful woman, though proud and overbearing, who could not bear to be surpassed in beauty by anyone. She had a magic looking-glass, and she used to stand before it, and look in it, and say,

"Looking-glass upon the wall,
Who is fairest of us all?"

And the looking-glass would answer,

"You are the fairest of them all."

She was contented, for she knew that the looking-glass spoke the truth.

Snow-white grew prettier and prettier, and when she was seven years old she was as beautiful as day, far more

128

beautiful than the queen herself. So one day when the queen went to her mirror and asked,

"Looking-glass upon the wall,
Who is fairest of us all?"

it answered,

"Queen you are full fair, 'tis true,
But Snow-white fairer is than you."

This gave the queen a great shock. She became yellow and green with envy, and from that hour her heart turned against Snow-white, and she hated her. Envy and pride grew like ill weeds higher in her heart with every day, until she had no peace day or night. At last she sent for a huntsman and said,

"Take the child out into the woods, so that I may set eyes on her no more. You must put her to death, and bring me her heart for a token."

The huntsman consented, and led her away; but when he drew his cutlass to pierce Snow-white's innocent heart, she began to weep, and to say,

"Oh, dear huntsman, do not take my life; I will go away into the wild wood and never come home again."

As she was so lovely the huntsman had pity on her, and said,

"Away with you then, poor child."

Just at that moment a young wild boar ran by. The huntsman caught and killed it, and taking out its heart, brought it to the queen for a token. The wicked woman ate it, thinking that now there was an end to Snow-white.

When the poor child found herself quite alone in the wild woods, she felt full of terror. She began to run over the sharp stones and through the thorn bushes, the wild beasts after her, but they did her no harm. When evening drew near she came to a little house and went inside to rest. She found everything in it very small, pretty and

clean. There stood a little table ready laid, covered with a white cloth, with seven little plates, and seven knives and forks, and drinking-cups. By the wall stood seven little beds, side by side, covered with white quilts. Snow-white, being hungry and thirsty, ate from each plate a little porridge and bread, and drank out of each little cup a drop of wine. After that she felt tired. She lay down on one of the beds, but it did not seem to suit her; one was too long, another short, but the seventh was just right; and so she lay down upon it and fell asleep.·

When it was quite dark, the masters of the house came home. They were seven dwarfs, whose occupation it was to dig under the mountains. When they had lit their seven candles they saw that someone must have come into their little house, as everything was not in the same order in which they left it. The first said,

"Who has been sitting in my little chair?"

The second said,

"Who has been eating from my little plate?"

The third said,

"Who has been taking my little loaf?"

The fourth said,

"Who has been tasting my porridge?"

The fifth said,

"Who has been using my little fork?"

The sixth said,

"Who has been cutting with my little knife?"

The seventh said,

"Who has been drinking from my little cup?"

Then the first one, looking round, saw a hollow in his bed, and cried,

"Who has been lying on my bed?"

And the others came running and cried,

"Someone has been on our beds too!"

But when the seventh looked at his bed, he saw little Snow-white lying there asleep. He told the others, who came running up, crying out in their astonishment, and holding up their seven little candles to throw a light upon Snow-white.

"O goodness! O gracious!" cried they. "What beautiful child is this?" They were so full of joy that they did not wake her, but let her sleep on. And the seventh dwarf slept with his comrades, an hour at a time with each, until the night had passed.

When it was morning, and Snow-white awoke and saw the seven dwarfs, she was very frightened. But they seemed quite friendly, and asked her what her name was. She told them; and then they asked how she came to be in their house. She told them that her step-mother had wished her to be put to death, and how the huntsman had spared her life. She added that she had run the whole day long, until at last she had found their little house. Then the dwarfs said,

"If you will keep our house for us, and cook, and wash, and make the beds, and sew and knit, and keep everything tidy and clean, you may stay with us, and you shall lack nothing."

"With all my heart," said Snow-white, and so she stayed, and kept the house in good order.

Every morning the dwarfs went to the mountain to dig for gold; in the evening they came home, and found their supper ready for them. All the day long the maiden was left alone. The good little dwarfs had warned her.

"Beware of your step-mother, she will soon know you are here. Let no one into the house."

The Queen, having eaten Snow-white's heart, as she supposed, felt quite sure that now she was the fairest. She came to her mirror, and asked,

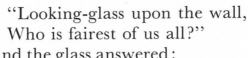

"Looking-glass upon the wall,
Who is fairest of us all?"
And the glass answered:
"Queen, thou art of beauty rare,
But Snow-white living in the glen
With the seven little men
Is a thousand times more fair."

She was then very angry, for the glass always spoke the truth. She knew that the huntsman must have deceived her, and that Snow-white must still be living. She thought and thought how to make an end of her, for as long as she was not the fairest in the land, she could have no rest.

At last she thought of a plan. She painted her face and dressed herself like an old pedlar woman, so that no one would have known her. In this disguise she went across the seven mountains, until she came to the house of the seven little dwarfs. She knocked at the door and cried,

"Fine wares to sell! Fine wares to sell!"

Snow-white peeped through the window and cried,

"Good-day, good woman, what have you to sell?"

"Good wares, fine wares," answered she, "laces of all colours," and she held up a piece that was woven of variegated silk.

"I need not be afraid of letting in this good woman," thought Snow-white, and she unbarred the door and bought the pretty lace.

"What a figure you are, child!" said the old woman, "come and let me lace you properly for once."

Snow-white, suspecting nothing, stood up before her, and let her lace her with the new lace; but the old woman laced so quick and tight that it took Snow-white's breath away, and she fell down as dead.

"Now you have done with being the fairest," said the

old woman as she hastened away.

Towards evening the seven dwarfs came home, and were terrified to see their dear Snow-white lying on the ground, without life or motion. They raised her up, and when they saw how tightly she was laced they cut the lace in two. She began to draw breath, and little by little she returned to life. When the dwarfs heard what had happened they said,

"The old pedlar woman was no other than the wicked queen; you must beware of letting any one in when we are not here!"

And when the wicked woman returned home she went to her glass and asked,

"Looking-glass against the wall,
Who is the fairest of us all?"

And it answered as before,

"Queen, thou art of beauty rare,
But Snow-white living in the glen
With the seven little men
Is a thousand times more fair."

When she heard that she was struck with surprise. She knew that Snow-white must still be living.

"But now," said she, "I will think of something that will be her ruin." By witchcraft she made a poisoned comb. Then she dressed herself to look like a different sort of old woman. She went across the seven mountains again and came to the house of the seven dwarfs. She knocked at the door and cried,

"Good wares to sell! Good wares to sell!"

Snow-white looked out and said,

"Go away, I must not let anybody in."

"But you are not forbidden to look," said the old woman, taking out the poisoned comb and holding it up. It pleased the poor child so much that she was tempted to

open the door; and when the bargain was made the old woman said,

"Now, for once your hair shall be properly combed."

Poor Snow-white, thinking no harm, let the old woman do as she would, but no sooner was the comb put in her hair than the poison began to work, and the poor girl fell down senseless.

"Now, you paragon of beauty," said the wicked woman, "this is the end of you." By good luck it was now near evening, and the seven little dwarfs soon came home. When they saw Snow-white lying on the ground as if dead, they thought directly that it was the step-mother's doing, and looked about. They found the poisoned comb, and no sooner had they drawn it out of her hair than Snow-white came to herself, and related all that had passed. They warned her once more to be on her guard, and let no one in at the door.

The queen went home and once more stood before the looking-glass and said,

"Looking-glass against the wall,
Who is fairest of all?"

And the looking-glass answered as before,

"Queen, thou art of beauty rare,
But Snow-white living in the glen
With the seven little men
Is a thousand times more fair."

When she heard the looking-glass speak thus, she trembled and shook with anger.

"Snow-white shall die," cried she, "though it should cost me my own life!"

She went then to a secret chamber and made a poisonous apple. It was beautiful to look upon, being white with red cheeks, so that anyone who should see it must long for it, but whoever ate even a little bit of it must

die. When the apple was ready she painted her face and clothed herself like a peasant woman, and went across the seven mountains to where the seven dwarfs lived. When she knocked at the door Snow-white put her head out of the window and said,

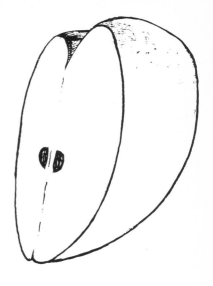

"I dare not let anybody in: the seven dwarfs told me not to."

"All right," answered the woman: "I can easily get rid of my apples elsewhere. There, I will give you one."

"No," answered Snow-white. "I dare not take any-thing."

"Are you afraid of poison?" said the woman. "Look here, I will cut the apple in two pieces; you shall have the red side, I will have the white one."

For the apple was so cunningly made, that all the poison was in the rosy half of it. Snow-white longed for the beautiful apple, and as she saw the peasant woman eating a piece of it she could no longer refrain, but stretched out her hand and took the poisoned half. No sooner had she taken a morsel of it into her mouth than she fell to the earth as if dead. And the queen, casting on her a terrible glance, laughed aloud and cried,

"As white as snow, as red as blood, as black as ebony! This time the dwarfs will not be able to bring you to life again."

And when she went home and asked the looking-glass,

"Looking-glass against the wall,
Who is fairest of us all?"

at last it answered,

"You are the fairest now of all."

Then her envious heart had peace, as much as an envious heart can have.

The dwarfs, when they came home in the evening, found Snow-white lying on the ground, and there came

no breath out of her mouth, and she was dead. They lifted her up, sought if anything poisonous was to be found, cut her laces, combed her hair, washed her with water and wine, but all was of no avail, the poor child was dead, and remained dead. Then they laid her on a bier, and sat all seven of them round it, and wept and lamented three whole days.

Snow-white looked as if she were living still, with her beautiful blooming cheeks. So they said,

"We cannot hide her away in the black ground." They had a coffin made of clear glass, so that it could be looked into from all sides. They laid her in it, and wrote her name upon it in golden letters, and that she was a king's daughter. Then they set the coffin out upon the mountain, with one of the dwarfs always remaining by it to watch. And the birds came too, and mourned for Snow-white, first an owl, then a raven, and lastly, a dove.

Now for a long while Snow-white lay in the coffin and never changed, but looked as if she were asleep, for she was still as white as snow, as red as blood, and her hair was as black as ebony. It happened, however, that one day a king's son rode through the wood and up to the dwarfs' house. On the mountain he saw the coffin, and beautiful Snow-white within it, and he read what was written upon it in golden letters. Then he said to the dwarfs,

"Let me have the coffin, and I will give you whatever you like to ask for it."

The dwarfs told him that they could not part with it for all the gold in the world, so he said,

"I beseech you to give it me, for I cannot live without looking upon Snow-white; if you consent I will bring you to great honour, and care for you as if you were my brethren."

When he spoke thus the good little dwarfs felt pity and

gave him the coffin. The king's son called his servants and bid them carry it away on their shoulders. Now it happened that as they were going along they stumbled over a bush, and with the shaking the bit of poisoned apple flew out of Snow-white's throat. It was not long before she opened her eyes, threw up the cover of the coffin, and sat up, alive and well.

"Oh dear! Where am I?" cried she. The king's son answered, full of joy, "You are near me," and relating all that had happened, he said,

"I would rather have you than anything in the world: come with me to my father's castle and you shall be my bride."

Snow-white liked him and went with him, so their wedding was held with pomp and great splendour.

But Snow-white's wicked step-mother was also bidden to the feast, and when she had dressed herself in beautiful clothes she went to her looking-glass and said,

"Looking-glass upon the wall,
Who is fairest of us all?"

The looking-glass answered,

"O Queen, although you are of beauty rare,
The young bride is a thousand times more fair."

Then she railed and cursed, and was beside herself with disappointment and anger. She felt she could have no peace until she went and saw the bride. And when she saw her she knew her for Snow-white, and could not stir from the place for anger and terror. For they had ready red-hot iron shoes, in which she had to dance until she fell down dead.

137

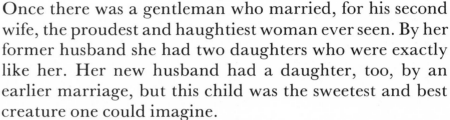

CHARLES PERRAULT

Cinderella

Once there was a gentleman who married, for his second wife, the proudest and haughtiest woman ever seen. By her former husband she had two daughters who were exactly like her. Her new husband had a daughter, too, by an earlier marriage, but this child was the sweetest and best creature one could imagine.

As soon as the wedding ceremony was over, the wife began to show her true nature. She could not bear it that her husband's pretty daughter with all her goodness made her own daughters appear the more hateful. She began to use her for the meanest housework. She ordered her to scour the pots and to scrub the tables and the floors. She gave her a wretched straw pallet for a bed in the garret while her own daughters lay below upon soft new beds and had full-length mirrors in which to admire themselves.

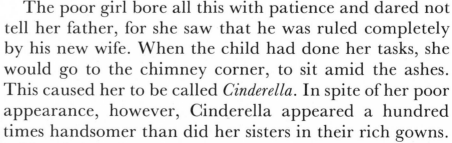

The poor girl bore all this with patience and dared not tell her father, for she saw that he was ruled completely by his new wife. When the child had done her tasks, she would go to the chimney corner, to sit amid the ashes. This caused her to be called *Cinderella*. In spite of her poor appearance, however, Cinderella appeared a hundred times handsomer than did her sisters in their rich gowns.

Now it happened that the King's son was giving a ball and invited to it all his fashionable friends. Thus the two

138

sisters of Cinderella received invitations and were filled with delight. At once they set about choosing gowns, petticoats, and head-dresses which would best suit them for the occasion. Cinderella had still more work to do now, for she was the one to iron their linen and plait their ruffles; and all day long she had to listen to their chatter about how they should be dressed.

The eldest girl said, "I shall wear my red velvet with the French trimming."

"And I," said the younger of the two, "shall wear my gold-flowered mantle and my diamond stomacher—which is far from ordinary."

Next they sent for the very best hairdresser to do up their hair.

Cinderella also had to be consulted about the hair-dressing, for the sisters knew she had excellent ideas. While she was helping them, they asked her, "Cinderella, would not you be glad also to go to the ball?"

"Ah, but you only joke," said Cinderella. "It is not for one such as I am to go to a ball."

"You are right," they replied. "People would laugh to see a Cinderella at a ball."

Anyone but Cinderella would have dealt roughly with them now, but she was so patient that she went on dressing them with the greatest care.

For almost two days the sisters were so transported by their joy that they could not bother to eat. They worked so hard trying to make their waists appear slender that they broke more than a dozen laces. And they paraded continually before their long mirrors.

At last the happy day arrived and they rode off to court. Cinderella looked after them as long as she could, and when they had gone out of sight she fell to crying.

Luckily, Cinderella had a fairy godmother who came

to her and was moved by her tears. "What is the matter?" she asked.

"I wish I could—I wish I could—" Cinderella was not able to go on, but her godmother understood and asked, "You wish you could go to the ball. Is that not so?"

"Y-yes," cried Cinderella, with a great sigh.

"Well now," said her godmother, "be but a good girl, and I shall see that you go."

She ordered Cinderella to run into the garden and get her a pumpkin.

Cinderella went at once to gather the finest pumpkin there was, though she could not imagine that this would enable her to go to the ball.

Her godmother took the pumpkin and scooped out the inside, leaving nothing but the shell. Then she struck it with her wand. Instantly it turned into an elegant coach, gilded all over with shining gold!

Now she went to a mouse-trap where she found six live mice. She ordered Cinderella to lift the door to the trap and as each mouse ran out she tapped it with her wand. Lo, each became a fine horse—all of them together a matched set in a beautiful, mouse-colour dapple-grey. They lacked only a coachman.

Cinderella had an idea. "I shall see if there is a rat in the rat-trap. We might make a coachman of him."

"You are right," replied her godmother. "Do go and look."

When Cinderella brought the rat-trap, there was indeed not one rat, but there were three huge ones! Her fairy godmother chose the one with the finest whiskers and touched him with her wand, whereupon there stood before them a fat, jolly coachman with the smartest beard ever beheld.

Now the fairy godmother ordered Cinderella to go into

the garden once more, to find six lizards behind the watering-pot.

Cinderella had no sooner returned with the lizards than these were turned into six footmen. They skipped behind the coach, their liveries shining with gold and silver, and they stayed in line as if they had always been footmen.

The fairy godmother now turned to Cinderella. "Well, you see here a carriage fit to take you to the ball. Are you not pleased?"

"Oh, yes, indeed," she cried. "But must I go in these horrid rags?"

Now it was Cinderella's turn to be tapped by the magic wand. At once her dingy rags became a gown of gold set with jewels, and her feet were shod with sparkling glass slippers.

Thus decked out, Cinderella climbed into her golden coach and was ready to set off. But before this was allowed, her godmother commanded her not to stay one moment after midnight. If she did, the coach would turn back into a pumpkin, her horses into mice, her coachman a rat, her footmen lizards, and her apparel again would be rags.

Cinderella promised her godmother that she would not fail to leave the ball before midnight. She drove off then, scarcely able to contain her joy.

At court, when the King's son was told that a great princess whom nobody recognized had come, he ran out to meet Cinderella. He gave her his hand as she alighted and with all ceremony led her into the hall among his guests. Everyone stopped dancing; the musicians ceased to play; each guest had to admire the extraordinary beauty of the unknown newcomer.

The King himself, old as he was, could not help watching her. He told his Queen that it had been a long

time since he had beheld so lovely a creature.

All the ladies began to study her gown and head-dress, planning to have them copied next day, if they could find such exquisite materials and so able a seamstress.

The Prince led Cinderella to a special seat and then took her to dance with him. So gracefully did she step and bow that they admired her all the more. When refreshments were served the Prince was so intent on gazing at her that he ate not a morsel himself.

Cinderella sat down by her sisters and even shared with them the special fruits and sweetmeats that the Prince had brought her. This surprised them indeed.

While Cinderella was thus amusing her sisters, suddenly she heard the clock strike eleven hours and three quarters. She got to her feet immediately, curtsied to the guests, and hastened away as fast as she could.

At home again, Cinderella sought out her godmother. After thanking her, she said she wished she might go next day to another ball, to which the Prince had invited her.

While she was telling her godmother all that had happened at the ball, Cinderella's two sisters knocked at the door.

"How long you have stayed," cried Cinderella as she opened the door, and she rubbed her eyes as if she had just awakened.

"Ah, but if you had been at the ball," said one of the sisters, "you would not have tired of it. There came to it the most beautiful princess ever seen. And she was kind to us, and generous, too. She shared her fruit and sweetmeats with us."

Cinderella asked them for the name of that princess. But she learned that they did not know and also that the King's son was anxious about the princess and would give everything to know her name.

At this, Cinderella smiled and replied, "She must be most beautiful, indeed. How happy you have been! Could I not see her, too? Ah, Charlotte, could not you lend me your yellow gown that you wear at home every day?"

"What! Lend my clothes to such a dirty Cinderella! I should be a fool!"

Cinderella well enough expected such an answer, and she was glad for it.

Next day the two sisters again went off to the ball, and so did Cinderella—dressed even more magnificently than before.

The King's son stayed by her side, never ceasing to pay her compliments and kindnesses, to the point that she forgot to watch the clock. The hour of twelve was striking when she thought it still no more than eleven. At once she arose and fled, as nimble as a deer.

The Prince followed Cinderella, but could not overtake her. However, he was able to pick up one of her glass slippers which had fallen off and been left behind.

Cinderella reached home quite out of breath, wearing her shabby old clothes, and holding one of the little slippers she had dropped.

The guards at the palace gate, when asked, said that they had not seen a princess go out. They had, however, seen a poor country girl, in very ragged clothes.

When the two sisters returned from the ball Cinderella asked them if they had been well entertained, and if the beautiful princess had come again.

They answered that she had been there but that she had hurried away when the clock struck twelve, and with such haste that she had dropped one of her little glass slippers, which the King's son had picked up. He had eyes for no one else at the ball and obviously was much

in love with the princess who owned the glass slipper.

This was all true. A few days later, the King's son proclaimed by trumpet that he sought to marry the one whose foot the slipper would fit. He was employing a servant to try it upon the princesses, the duchesses, and the other court ladies—but in vain.

When the time came for each of her sisters to try the slipper, Cinderella stood by and watched. Knowing that it was her slipper, she finally said, "Let me see if it will fit me."

Her sisters burst out laughing. But the servant with the slipper looked at Cinderella and said that she should try. Furthermore, he had been ordered to let everyone put on the slipper.

He asked Cinderella to sit down and, sliding the slipper on to her foot, found it a perfect fit. The sisters were astonished, and even more so when Cinderella pulled out of her pocket the matching slipper and put it on her other foot.

Thereupon, in came the godmother who once more touched Cinderella's clothes with her wand and made them even richer than those she had worn before.

Now Cinderella's two sisters saw that she was the beautiful girl they had seen at the ball. They threw themselves at her feet to beg pardon for their ill treatment of her. As Cinderella embraced her sisters, she cried out that she forgave them entirely, and desired them always to love her. She herself was led to the young Prince who found her more charming than ever. And in a few days he married her.

Because Cinderella was no less good than she was beautiful, she gave her sisters rooms in the palace and even arranged marriages between them and two of the lords of the Court.

CHARLES PERRAULT

Little Red Riding-Hood

Once upon a time there lived a little country girl who was the prettiest ever seen. Her mother was immensely fond of her, and her grandmother, who loved her even more, made for her a little red riding-hood. This suited the little girl so well that everybody then called her Little Red Riding-Hood.

One day her mother, having made some custards, said to Little Red Riding-Hood, "Go, my dear, and see how your grandmamma is feeling. She has been ill. Take her this custard and this little pot of butter."

Little Red Riding-Hood set out at once to go to her grandmother, who lived in another village.

As she was skipping through the wood, Little Red Riding-Hood met a wolf. The beast had a mind to eat her up at once, but he dared not because of some wood-cutters nearby in the forest. But he stopped her to ask her where she was going. Little Red Riding-Hood, who did not know that it was dangerous to listen to a wolf, said to him, "I am going to see my grandmamma and carry her a custard and a little pot of butter from my mamma."

"Does she live far off?" asked the wolf.

"Oh, yes," answered Little Red Riding-Hood. "She lives beyond that mill you see there, in the first house in the village."

"Well," said the wolf. "I'll go and see her, too. I'll

go this way and you go that. We shall see who will get there first."

The wolf began to run as fast as he could, taking the nearest path. The little girl went by the longer route, and she stopped to gather nuts, run after butterflies, and pick flowers for a nosegay.

The wolf soon came to the old woman's house and knocked at the door—tap, tap.

"Who is there?" called an old woman's voice.

"It is your grandchild, Little Red Riding-Hood," answered the wolf, disguising his voice. "I've brought you a custard and a little pot of butter from mamma."

The good grandmother, who was still in bed because she was ill, cried out, "Pull the bobbin, and the latch will go up."

The wolf pulled the bobbin and the door opened. At once he fell upon the the good woman and gobbled her down in a moment, for it had been more than three days since he had eaten. He then shut the door and lay in the grandmother's bed to await Little Red Riding-Hood.

Some time afterwards Little Red Riding-Hood knocked at the door—tap, tap.

"Who is there?"

Little Red Riding-Hood, hearing the big voice of the wolf, was at first afraid but she believed that her grandmother had a cold and thus was hoarse, so she answered, "It is your granddaughter, Little Red Riding-Hood. I have brought you a custard and a little pot of butter from mamma."

Softening his voice as much as he could, the wolf cried out now, "Pull the bobbin, and the latch will go up."

Little Red Riding-Hood pulled the bobbin, and the door opened.

The wolf, seeing her come in, said to her, as he hid under

the bedclothes, "Put the custard and the little pot of butter upon the stool, and come lie down with me."

Little Red Riding-Hood came to the bed. But, seeing how strangely her grandmother looked, she said to her, "Grandmamma, what great arms you have!"

"All the better to hug you with, my dear."

"Grandmamma, what great ears you have!"

"All the better to hear you with, my dear."

"Grandmamma, what great eyes you have!"

"All the better to see you with, my dear."

"Grandmamma, what great teeth you have!"

"All the better to eat you with, my dear."

And with these words, the wicked wolf fell upon Little Red Riding-Hood, and ate her up.

Now the wolf, having satisfied his hunger, went to sleep, snoring loudly. He snored so very loudly, indeed, that a hunter passing the house decided to enter to see if there was something wrong with the old woman.

When he walked up to her bed, he found the wolf. "Aha," he said, "I have been looking for you a long time." He saw that the wolf must have swallowed the grandmother and that she might yet be saved. He picked up a pair of shears and began to slit open the wolf's body. After a few snips, Little Red Riding-Hood appeared, and after a few more, out she jumped. Then out came the old grandmother.

All three were pleased. The huntsman took off the wolf's skin, and carried it home. The grandmother ate the custard, and Little Red Riding-Hood said she would never more pick flowers in the wood or listen to a wolf.

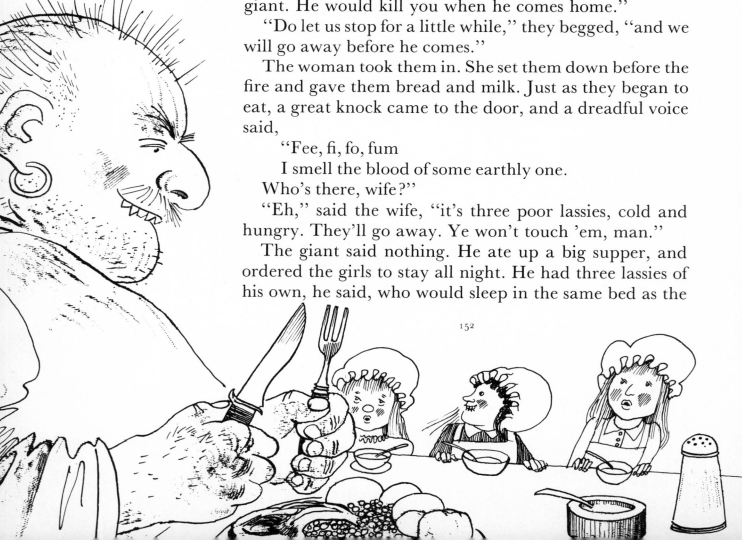

Molly Whuppie

Once upon a time a man and his wife had too many children. They could not feed them all, so they took the three youngest and left them in a wood. The three little girls walked and walked, but never a house could they see. It began to be dark, and they were hungry.

At last the little girls saw a light and headed for it. It shone from a house. They rapped on the door, and a woman came, who said, "What do you want?"

"Please let us in and give us something to eat."

The woman answered, "I can't do that, as my man is a giant. He would kill you when he comes home."

"Do let us stop for a little while," they begged, "and we will go away before he comes."

The woman took them in. She set them down before the fire and gave them bread and milk. Just as they began to eat, a great knock came to the door, and a dreadful voice said,

"Fee, fi, fo, fum
I smell the blood of some earthly one.
Who's there, wife?"

"Eh," said the wife, "it's three poor lassies, cold and hungry. They'll go away. Ye won't touch 'em, man."

The giant said nothing. He ate up a big supper, and ordered the girls to stay all night. He had three lassies of his own, he said, who would sleep in the same bed as the three strangers. Now the youngest of the three girls was called Molly Whuppie, and she was very clever. She noticed that before they went to bed the giant put straw ropes round her neck and her sisters', and round his own daughters' necks he put gold chains. So Molly took care not to fall asleep, but waited till she was sure everyone was sleeping sound.

Then Molly slipped out of bed. She took the straw ropes off her own and her sisters' necks, and took the gold chains off the giant's lassies. She then put the straw ropes on the giant's daughters and the gold ones on herself and her sisters, and lay down.

In the middle of the night up rose the giant, and he felt for the necks with the straw. It was dark. He took his own daughters out of bed, and carried them out to a cage where he locked them up. Then he lay down again.

Molly thought it was time she and her sisters were off and away. She woke them and told them to be quiet, and they slipped out of the house. They all got out safe, and they ran and ran.

They never stopped until morning, when they saw a grand house before them.

It turned out to be a King's house, so Molly went in and told her story to the King. The King said, "Well, Molly, you are a clever girl. You have managed well. But – you can manage better yet. Go back and steal the giant's sword that hangs on the back of his bed, and I'll give your eldest sister my eldest son to marry."

Molly said she would try. So she went back. She managed to slip into the giant's house and hide under his bed.

The giant came home, ate up a great supper, and went to bed. Molly waited until he was snoring. Then she crept out and reached over the giant and got down the

sword. But just as she got it out over the bed, the sword gave a rattle. Up jumped the giant!

Molly ran out the door, and took the sword with her. She ran, and he ran, till they came to the "Bridge of One Hair". She got over, but he couldn't; and he cried, "Woe unto ye, Molly Whuppie, if ye ever come here again!"

But Molly replied, "Twice yet I'll come to Spain."

So Molly took the sword to the King, and her sister was wed to his son.

Well, the King said, "You've managed well, Molly. But you can do better yet. Go back and steal the purse that lies below the giant's pillow, and I'll marry your second sister to my second son."

Molly said she would try. So she set out for the giant's house and slipped in and hid again under his bed. She waited till the giant had eaten his supper and was sound asleep snoring.

She crept out then. She slipped her hand under the pillow, and got out the purse. But, just as she was leaving the giant wakened, and ran after her.

She ran, and he ran, till they came to the "Bridge of One Hair". She got over, but he couldn't; and he cried, "Woe unto ye, Molly Whuppie, if ye ever come here again!"

But Molly replied, "Once yet I'll come to Spain."

So Molly took the purse to the King, and her second sister was wed to the King's second son.

After that the King said to Molly, "Molly, you are a clever girl. But you can do better yet. Steal the giant's ring that he wears on his finger, and I'll give you my youngest son for yourself."

Molly said she would try. So back she went to the giant's house and hid under the bed. The giant wasn't long in coming home. After he had eaten a great supper, he went to his bed, and shortly was snoring loud.

Molly crept out and reached over the bed. She took hold of the giant's hand. She pulled and she pulled at the ring on his finger. But just as she got it off the giant rose up, and gripped her by the hand. "Now I have caught ye, Molly Whuppie! Well, now – if I had done as much ill to ye as ye have done to me, what would ye do to me?"

At once Molly said, "I would put you into a sack. I'd put the cat inside with you, and the dog beside you, and a needle and thread and shears. And I'd hang you up upon the wall. Then I'd go to the wood, and I would choose the biggest stick I could get. I would come home and take you down and bang you till you were dead."

"Well, Molly," said the giant, "I'll do just that to ye."

So he got a sack, and put Molly into it, and the cat and the dog beside her, with a needle and thread and shears. He hung her up upon the wall. Then he went to the wood to choose a stick.

Molly sang out, "Oh, if you saw what I see!"

"Oh," said the giant's wife, "what do you see, Molly?"

156

But Molly never said a word, only, "Oh, if you saw what I see!"

The giant's wife begged Molly to take her up into the sack so she could see what Molly saw. So Molly took the shears and cut a hole in the sack. She took the needle and thread out with her, and jumped down and helped the giant's wife up into the sack, and sewed up the hole.

The giant's wife saw nothing, and began to ask to get down again. But Molly never minded. She hid herself behind the door. Home came the giant with a big tree in his hand. He took down the sack and began to batter it. His wife cried out, "It's me, man, it's me, man!" But the dog barked so, and the cat mewed so, that the giant did not hear his wife's voice.

Molly came out from behind the door. The giant saw her and ran after her. He ran, and she ran, till they came to the "Bridge of One Hair." She got over, but he couldn't; and he said, "Woe unto ye, Molly Whuppie, if ye ever come here again."

But Molly replied, "Never more will I come to Spain!"

So Molly took the ring to the King. She was married to his youngest son, and she never saw the giant again.

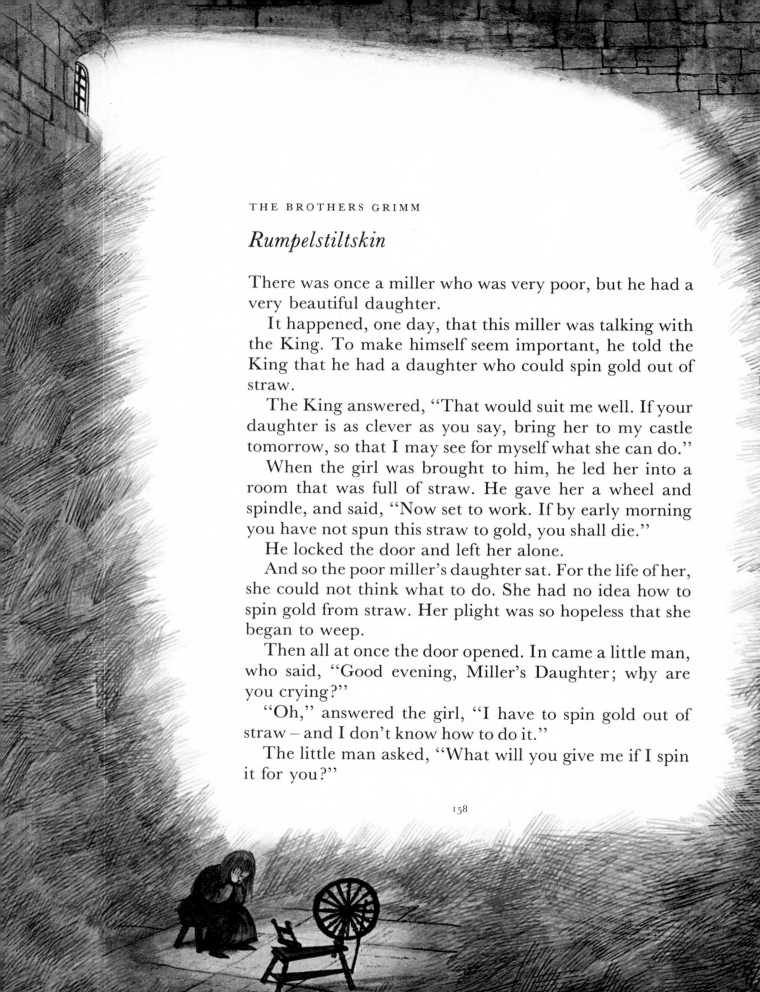

THE BROTHERS GRIMM

Rumpelstiltskin

There was once a miller who was very poor, but he had a very beautiful daughter.

It happened, one day, that this miller was talking with the King. To make himself seem important, he told the King that he had a daughter who could spin gold out of straw.

The King answered, "That would suit me well. If your daughter is as clever as you say, bring her to my castle tomorrow, so that I may see for myself what she can do."

When the girl was brought to him, he led her into a room that was full of straw. He gave her a wheel and spindle, and said, "Now set to work. If by early morning you have not spun this straw to gold, you shall die."

He locked the door and left her alone.

And so the poor miller's daughter sat. For the life of her, she could not think what to do. She had no idea how to spin gold from straw. Her plight was so hopeless that she began to weep.

Then all at once the door opened. In came a little man, who said, "Good evening, Miller's Daughter; why are you crying?"

"Oh," answered the girl, "I have to spin gold out of straw – and I don't know how to do it."

The little man asked, "What will you give me if I spin it for you?"

"My necklace," answered the girl.

The little man took the necklace. He sat down before the wheel, and – *whirr, whirr, whirr!* – three times round, and the bobbin was full of gold. Then he took up another, and – *whirr, whirr, whirr!* – three times round, and that one was full. So he went on till the morning, when all the straw was spun and all the bobbins were full of gold.

At sunrise, in came the King. When he saw the gold, he was astonished – and very pleased, for he was greedy. He had the miller's daughter taken into another room filled with straw, much bigger than the last. He told her that if she wanted to live she must spin all this in one night.

Again the girl did not know what to do, so she began to cry. The door opened, and the same little man appeared as before. He asked, "What will you give me if I spin all this straw into gold?"

"The ring from my finger," answered the girl.

So the little man took the ring, and began again to send the wheel whirring round.

By the next morning all the straw was spun into glittering gold. The King was happy beyond words. But, as he could never have enough gold, he had the miller's daughter taken into a still larger room full of straw, and said, "This straw, too, you must spin in one night. If you do, you shall be my wife." He thought to himself, "Although she is but a miller's daughter, I am not likely to find anyone richer in the whole world."

As soon as the girl was alone, the little man came for the third time and asked, "What will you give me if I spin this straw for you?"

"I have nothing left to give," answered the girl.

"Then you must promise me the first child you have after you are Queen," said the little man.

"Well, who knows what may happen?" thought the girl. As she could think of nothing else to do, she promised the little man what he demanded. In return, he began to spin, and spun until all the straw was gold.

In the morning when the King came and found everything done as he wished, he had the wedding held at once, and the miller's pretty daughter became Queen.

In a year's time, a beautiful child was born. The Queen had forgotten all about the little man – until one day he came into her room suddenly and said, "Now give me what you promised me."

The Queen was terrified. She offered the little man all the riches of the kingdom – if only he would leave the child.

But the little man said, "No, I would rather have a living baby than all the treasures of the world."

The Queen began to weep, so that the little man felt sorry for her.

"I will give you three days," he said, "and if in that time you cannot tell my name, you must give me the child."

The Queen spent the whole night thinking over all the names she had ever heard. She sent a messenger through the land to ask far and wide for all the names that could be found.

When the little man came next day, she began with Caspar, Melchior, and Balthazar, and she repeated all she knew.

But after each the little man said, "No, that is not my name."

The second day the Queen sent to ask all the neighbours what their servants were called. She told the little man all the most unusual names, saying, "Perhaps you are called Cow-ribs, or Sheep-shanks, or Spider-legs?"

But he answered only, "No, that is not my name."

On the third day the messenger came back and said, "I have not been able to find one single new name. But as I passed through the woods, I came to a high hill. Near it was a little house, and before the house burned a fire. Around the fire danced a funny little man, who hopped on one leg and sang:

"Tomorrow at last the child comes in,
For nobody knows I'm Rumpelstiltskin."

You cannot think how pleased the Queen was to hear that name!

Soon the little man himself walked in and asked, "Now, Your Majesty, what is my name?"

At first she asked, "Are you called Jack?"

"No, that is not my name."

"Are you called Harry?"

"No," answered he.

And then she asked, "Perhaps your name is Rumpel-stiltskin?"

"The devil told you that! The devil told you that!" shrieked the little man. In his anger he stamped with his right foot so hard that it went into the ground above his knee. Then he seized his left foot with both hands in such a fury that he split in two. And that was the end of him!

One-Inch Fellow

Once upon a time there lived an old man and an old woman in the village of Naniwa, which is the present city of Osaka. They were a happy couple, except for one thing. They had no child to cheer their lonely old age.

One afternoon they went to the temple and prayed, "Please, god of mercy, give us a child – any child, even if it be as small as a thumb."

On a summer evening after this, as the old couple were looking up at a beautiful moon, they saw something strange, like a spot of darkness coming at them from the moon. It came nearer and nearer, and soon seemed to them like a purple cloud.

The cloud floated into the room where the old man and old woman were sitting. It twirled and untwirled itself, and quickly wafted away again. The old couple watched in silent wonder and then with great joy, for the purple cloud had left behind it a tiny boy as small as a thumb.

This gift was received as a miracle by the grateful couple. They soon discovered that the little fellow did not grow bigger as babies do, but they continued to be grateful and to care lovingly for the tiny boy. He remained as small as a thumb, so the old couple named him "One-Inch Fellow".

Whenever One-Inch Fellow ventured out on the street alone, the good old woman worried. "Old man, old man, what if the children on the street should fight with One-Inch Fellow? He would be crushed!"

But she need not have worried. Whenever the teasing children came toward One-Inch Fellow, he would dart away quick as a flash between their wooden clogs, so that they could not find him.

Fourteen summers went by and One-Inch Fellow was now a young man.

"Honourable Father, honourable Mother," he said one day, bowing low before his parents. They were seated at their low table, which to One-Inch Fellow seemed like a high roof above him.

The old man looked down upon his son. "What is it, my son?"

"I should like your permission to go to the capital of Kyoto to make a name for myself."

"And why is that?" asked the parents in surprise.

"Because I am a grown son now," he answered, lifting his tiny head high. "My gratitude to you is higher than the highest mountains and deeper than the deepest seas. I want to make a name for myself so that you will be proud of me."

The old man looked down. "I give you permission. Go, my son!"

During the next days, the old parents were very busy. The old woman made a new kimono for One-Inch Fellow. "In Kyoto young men dress with style. I shall have my son look his best."

The old man also planned for his son. "He is too small for a real boat. And he must have a sword. No son of mine can step out into the world without a sword."

Early on the day of departure, the old woman was up, cooking over her charcoal fire, while the old man prepared a farewell speech. In silence the three ate their breakfast

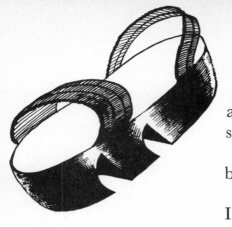

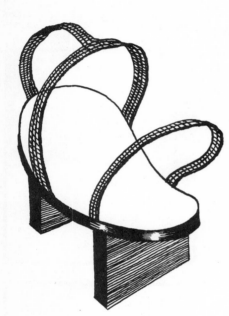

and One-Inch Fellow neatly tied in his little square cloth some newly cooked rice balls and salted plums.

"Honourable parents, I take my leave now," he said, bowing low before them.

"This is your sword," said his father, handing to One-Inch Fellow a shiny, sharp needle in a scabbard of straw. "Keep it always stainless like your soul.

"And this is your boat," added his father, placing a black lacquered soup bowl with one chopstick before him. "Steer it well to Kyoto with this oar. And now go, my son."

Carrying the boat, the parents walked with One-Inch Fellow to the water's edge. The old man put the bowl on the water and helped his son climb into it. With his oar One-Inch Fellow steered his boat out to the deeper part of the river. The voices of the old people called after him as he paddled away. "*Banzai! Banzai!*"

The old man continued to wave, but the old woman hid her face in her sleeve.

One-Inch Fellow started thus on his way to a famous career. With his chopstick paddle he pushed on and on. Angry waves sometimes threw him clear off his course. One stormy day he hid behind a support of a bridge and rested until the wind died and there was only a gentle breeze.

Finally one morning early he saw the city of Kyoto rising in the mist. Happily he steered toward shore. He stepped out of his boat, and he pushed it away. "When I return to Naniwa," he said, "I shall have an attendant and shall not need this little boat."

Compared to his quiet home of Naniwa, One-Inch Fellow found the capital big and noisy. He walked briskly down the middle of a wide street where crowds of people passed back and forth. No one noticed so tiny a

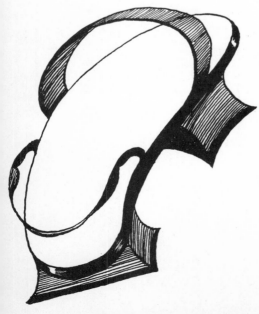

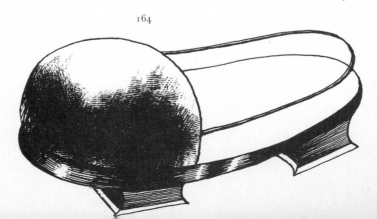

fellow. After passing several wooden gates, One-Inch Fellow stopped before the highest and longest walls. "This must be a rich household. I shall offer my services here."

Through the largest gateway he made his way and, walking over a long road, came finally to the entrance of an immense mansion. It belonged to a famous lord of Kyoto. On the great stone step at the door, he saw a pair of shiny painted black shoes. The lord of the mansion was about to go out.

"Hear me!" One-Inch Fellow shouted as loud as he could.

"Who is that?" It was the dignified lord himself who answered.

"It is I, a youth from Naniwa," answered One-Inch Fellow.

The lord came out and looked around, but he could not see anyone.

Again One-Inch Fellow shouted, "Here I am!"
The startled lord looked down at the ground.

"*Yo!* What a tiny fellow; but you have a mighty voice! Who are you?"

"I am called One-Inch Fellow. I have come all the way from Naniwa to serve a great lord."

"*Yo!* I do not know what a little fellow like you could do."

"But," cried One-Inch Fellow, "you will find no other fellow like me on all this earth!"

"That is so! All right, you may serve me," said the lord.

From that day, One-inch Fellow became a faithful servant to this lord of Kyoto. He was given the duty of cleaning all the shiny lacquered shoes. In his spare moments he never failed to clear away a fallen leaf or a stray pine needle from the mossy ground. Always he was

courteous and bright and did willingly any errands asked of him. The whole household liked to call out, "One-Inch Fellow! One-Inch Fellow!" In the servants' hall he became a much sought-after little man.

At length One-Inch Fellow won the attention of the beautiful Princess, who was the only daughter of the lord. He became such a favourite with her, in fact, that the lord permitted him to be her bodyguard. Every winter he went out with her to celebrate the New Year. In the spring he accompanied her to the cherry-blossom festivals; and in summer he shared in the viewing of the full moon. When fall came, One-Inch Fellow escorted the Princess, with other attendants, to the shrine of Ise, where every maiden makes a holy pilgrimage at least once before her marriage.

This pilgrimage was such a long journey that One-Inch Fellow sometimes rode in the pocket of another attendant.

After the visit to the shrine the Princess, with One-Inch Fellow and her other attendants close behind her, came down a long, shadowy avenue of cedar trees. Suddenly a huge monster, an *Oni*, leaped out of the darkness, yelling, "*Wa – ! Wa – !*"

At the sight of this ugly *Oni*, the beautiful Princess screamed, and fainted away, while the terrified attendants ran off in different directions to hide. Only tiny One-Inch Fellow stood his ground.

"What are you?" he shouted, standing before the Princess. "Do you know who I am!" he cried, looking up to the fierce *Oni*. "I am the famous One-Inch Fellow who serves the great lord of Kyoto. This is his only daughter. If you even so much as come near her, beware!"

"Ha! Ha! Ha! I like to hear you talk!" laughed the huge *Oni*, looking down at the tiny man. "But that is enough. Do not bother me, or I shall eat you up!"

"*Yoshi!* Go ahead," cried One-Inch Fellow, angrily.

As One-Inch Fellow expected, the huge monster
caught hold of him, and started to put him into his huge
mouth. Quickly One-Inch Fellow darted on to his cheek.
He climbed up to the monster's eye, whipped out his
needle sword, and thrust it at the eye.

"*Itai!* Ouch!" cried the monster, trying to catch him.
But One-Inch Fellow slipped from the monster's fingers
and went on thrusting his needle sword all over the *Oni's*
face.

"No more! No more!" roared the monster. "I make my
humble bow to you!"

One-Inch Fellow quickly ran down to the ground and

the *Oni* disappeared into the shadows. By this time the Princess had opened her eyes. "What happened to the *Oni*?" she asked.

"I have chased him away with my sword. Do not worry, Princess. One-Inch Fellow, your bodyguard, is at your service."

Then the Princess exclaimed, "What is that?"

A few feet away lay a large wooden hammer.

"That must be something the monster left behind," said One-Inch Fellow. "If you are rested, let us hasten homeward."

"Wait!" cried the Princess, lifting up the hammer. "Stand there, One-Inch Fellow. This looks like a magic hammer that can answer wishes. That monster must have been a god in disguise who came to test you. Otherwise he would not have left behind this precious hammer."

"May I ask, Princess, how you know that is such a wonderful gift?"

"We shall see," said the Princess solemnly. One-Inch Fellow had never seen the Princess so solemn.

"If this be the magic hammer my honoured father has spoken of, then when you strike it, anything you wish will come true. What do you wish, One-Inch Fellow? Speak!"

"I have nothing to wish for since my wish has been granted. I am serving your honoured father. Still – perhaps I might like to be a little taller."

"Please, merciful god, make One-Inch Fellow tall as a man." The Princess said this very quietly, and struck the hammer on the ground.

Strange! Strange! One-Inch Fellow seemed to see the earth sinking lower and lower. But it was not the earth that was changing; it was he who was growing taller.

"Please, merciful god, make him tall as a man," the Princess said, as she struck the hammer a second time.

168

As she repeated this for the third time, the Princess smiled at One-Inch Fellow. She lifted the hammer into the air and let it fall to the ground again with a heavy thud.

The beautiful Princess now went to her little travelling box which an attendant had thrown down before he ran away. From it she took a round mirror, which she held toward One-Inch Fellow. Looking into the mirror, he saw that he was tall! The Princess lifted the mirror higher and higher so that he could see himself all the way from the tips of his feet to his manly face. He was not merely tall – he was magnificent, a full six feet!

With joy in their hearts, the Princess and the tall youth returned to her father's mansion. For saving the life of his precious daughter, the lord promoted the lad to a high rank, while the cowardly attendants who had fled at the sight of the monster resigned from their positions in great shame. News of the brave youth who had saved the life of the Princess became gossip in every corner of the court. Finally the heroic story even reached the gracious ears of the Emperor, and the youth was immediately summoned before him. The Emperor bestowed a high title on One-Inch Fellow and not long after gave him an honourable position.

Before three full moons had passed, the youth dressed in his full court regalia and went to see his honoured parents. Behind him on the journey followed his attendants and two palanquins which were to carry his parents back to the beautiful home which the youth had had built for himself in Kyoto. The old couple were made very happy, sharing the honours of their son. But they were happy, above all, because the youth was no longer as tiny as a thumb. Their old feet were never too weary to take them to the temple, to offer their prayers of gratitude.

HANS CHRISTIAN ANDERSEN

The Real Princess

There was once a prince, and he wanted a princess, but then she must be a *real* princess. He travelled right round the world to find one, but there was always something wrong. There were plenty of princesses, but whether they were real princesses he had great difficulty in discovering; there was always something which was not quite right about them. So at last he had to come home again, and he was very sad because he wanted a real princess so badly.

One evening there was a terrible storm; it thundered and lightninged and the rain poured down in torrents; indeed it was a fearful night.

In the middle of the storm somebody knocked at the town gate, and the old king himself went to open it.

It was a princess who stood outside, but she was in a terrible state from the rain and the storm. The water streamed out of her hair and her clothes, it ran in at the top of her shoes and out at the heel, but she said that she was a real princess.

"Well, we shall soon see if that is true," thought the old queen, but she said nothing. She went into the bedroom, took all the bedclothes off and laid a pea on the bedstead; then she took twenty mattresses and piled them on the top of the pea, and then twenty feather beds on the top of the mattresses. This was where the princess was to sleep that night. In the morning they asked her how she had slept.

"Oh, terribly badly!" said the princess. "I have hardly closed my eyes the whole night! Heaven knows what was in the bed. I seemed to be lying upon some hard thing, and my whole body is black and blue this morning. It is terrible!"

They saw at once that she must be a real princess when she had felt the pea through twenty mattresses and twenty feather beds. Nobody but a real princess could have such a delicate skin.

So the prince took her to be his wife, for now he was sure that he had found a real princess, and the pea was put into the Museum, where it may still be seen if no one has stolen it.

Now this is a true story.

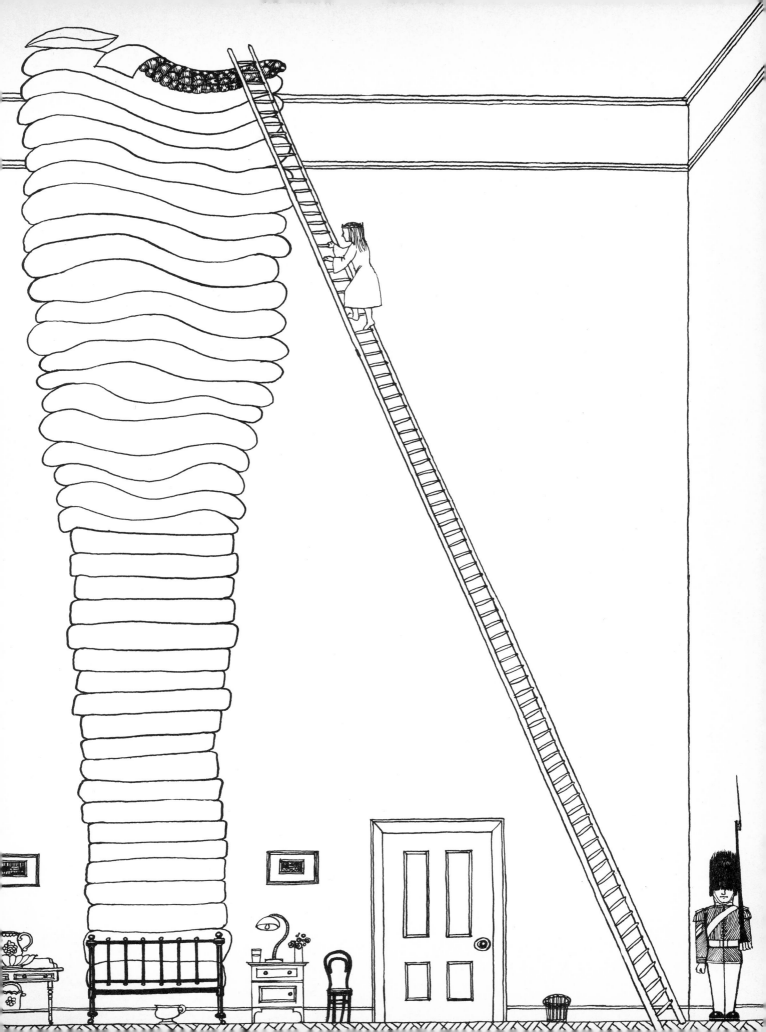

HANS CHRISTIAN ANDERSEN

The Emperor's New Clothes

Many years ago there was an emperor who was so excessively fond of new clothes that he spent all his money upon them. He cared nothing about his soldiers nor for the theatre, nor for driving in the woods except for the sake of showing off his new clothes. He had a costume for every hour in the day and instead of saying as one does about any other king or emperor, "He is in his council chamber," here one always said, "The emperor is in his dressing-room."

Life was very gay in the great town where he lived; hosts of strangers came to visit it every day, and among them one day two swindlers. They gave themselves out as weavers, and said that they knew how to weave the most beautiful stuffs imaginable. Not only were the colours and patterns unusually fine, but the clothes that were made of the stuffs had the peculiar quality of becoming invisible to every person who was not fit for the office he held, or if he was impossibly dull.

"Those must be splendid clothes," thought the emperor. "By wearing them I should be able to discover which men in my kingdom are unfitted for their posts. I shall distinguish the wise men from the fools. Yes, I certainly must order some of that stuff to be woven for me."

He paid the two swindlers a lot of money in advance so that they might begin their work at once.

They did put up two looms and pretended to weave, but they had nothing whatever upon their shuttles. At the outset they asked for a quantity of the finest silk and the purest gold thread, all of which they put into their own bags while they worked away at the empty looms far into the night.

"I should like to know how those weavers are getting on with the stuff," thought the emperor; but he felt a little queer when he reflected that anyone who was stupid or unfit for his post would not be able to see it. He certainly thought that he need have no fears for himself, but still he thought he would send somebody else first to see how it was getting on. Everybody in the town knew what wonderful power the stuff possessed, and everyone was anxious to see how stupid his neighbour was.

"I will send my faithful old minister to the weavers," thought the emperor. "He will be best able to see how the stuff looks, for he is a clever man and no one fulfils his duties better than he does."

So the good old minister went into the room where the two swindlers sat working at the empty loom.

"Heaven preserve us!" thought the old minister, opening his eyes very wide. "Why, I can't see a thing!" But he took care not to say so.

Both the swindlers begged him to be good enough to step a little nearer, and asked if he did not think it a good pattern and beautiful colouring. They pointed to the empty loom, and the poor old minister stared as hard as he could but he could not see anything, for of course there was nothing to see.

"Good Heavens!" thought he, "is it possible that I am a fool. I have never thought so and nobody must know it. Am I not fit for my post? It will never do to say that I cannot see the stuff."

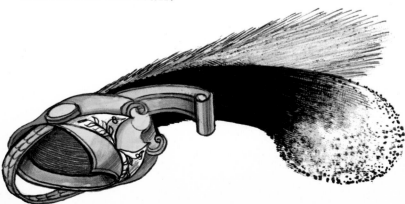

"Well, sir, you don't say anything about the stuff," said the one who was pretending to weave.

"Oh, it is beautiful! quite charming!" said the old minister looking through his spectacles; "this pattern and these colours! I will certainly tell the emperor that the stuff pleases me very much."

"We are delighted to hear you say so," said the swindlers, and then they named all the colours and described the peculiar pattern. The old minister paid great attention to what they said, so as to be able to repeat it when he got home to the emperor.

Then the swindlers went on to demand more money, more silk, and more gold thread, to be able to proceed with the weaving; but they put it all into their own pockets – not a single strand was ever put into the loom, but they went on as before weaving at the empty loom.

The emperor soon sent another faithful official to see how the stuff was getting on, and if it would soon be ready. The same thing happened to him as to the minister; he looked and looked, but as there was only the empty loom, he could see nothing at all.

"Is not this a beautiful piece of stuff?" said both the swindlers, showing and explaining the beautiful pattern and colours which were not there to be seen.

"I know I am not a fool!" thought the man, "so it must be that I am unfit for my good post! It is very strange though! however one must not let it appear!" So he praised the stuff he did not see, and assured them of his delight in the beautiful colours and the originality of the design. "It is absolutely charming!" he said to the emperor. Everybody in the town was talking about this splendid stuff.

Now the emperor thought he would like to see it while it was still on the loom. So, accompanied by a number of

176

selected courtiers, among whom were the two faithful officials who had already seen the imaginary stuff, he went on to visit the crafty impostors, who were working away as hard as ever they could at the empty loom.

"It is magnificent!" said both the officials. "Only see, Your Majesty, what a design! What colours!" And they pointed to the empty loom, for they thought no doubt the others could see the stuff.

"What!" thought the emperor; "I see nothing at all! This is terrible! Am I a fool? Am I not fit to be emperor? Why, nothing worse could happen to me!"

"Oh, it is beautiful!" said the emperor. "It has my highest approval!" and he nodded his satisfaction as he gazed at the empty loom. Nothing would induce him to say that he could not see anything.

The whole suite gazed and gazed, but saw nothing more than all the others. However, they all exclaimed with His Majesty: "It is very beautiful!" and they advised him to wear a suit made of this wonderful cloth on the occasion of a great procession which was just about to take place. "It is magnificent! Gorgeous! Excellent!" went from mouth to mouth; they were all equally delighted with it. The emperor gave each of the rogues an order of knighthood to be worn in their buttonholes and the title of "Gentlemen Weavers".

The swindlers sat up the whole night, before the day on which the procession was to take place, burning sixteen candles; so that people might see how anxious they were to get the emperor's new clothes ready. They pretended to take the stuff off the loom. They cut it out in the air with a huge pair of scissors, and they stitched away with needles without any thread in them. At last they said: "Now the emperor's new clothes are ready!"

The emperor, with his grandest courtiers, went to them

177

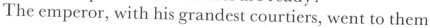

himself, and both the swindlers raised one arm in the air, as if they were holding something, and said: "See, these are the trousers, this is the coat, here is the mantle!" and so on. "It is as light as a spider's web. One might think one had nothing on, but that is the very beauty of it!"

"Yes!" said all the courtiers, but they could not see anything, for there was nothing to see.

"Will Your Imperial Majesty be graciously pleased to take off your clothes," said the impostors, "so that we may put on the new ones, along here before the great mirror."

The emperor took off all his clothes, and the impostors pretended to give him one article of dress after the other, of the new ones which they had pretended to make. They pretended to fasten something round his waist and to tie on something; this was the train, and the emperor turned round and round in front of the mirror.

"How well His Majesty looks in the new clothes! How becoming they are," cried all the people round. "What a design, and what colours! They are most gorgeous robes!"

"The canopy is waiting outside which is to be carried over Your Majesty in the procession," said the master of ceremonies.

"Well, I am quite ready," said the emperor. "Don't the clothes fit well?" and then he turned round again in front of the mirror, so that he should seem to be looking at his grand things.

The chamberlains who were to carry the train stooped and pretended to lift it from the ground with both hands, and they walked along with their hands in the air. They dared not let it appear that they could not see anything.

Then the emperor walked along in the procession under the gorgeous canopy, and everybody in the streets and at the windows exclaimed. "How beautiful the

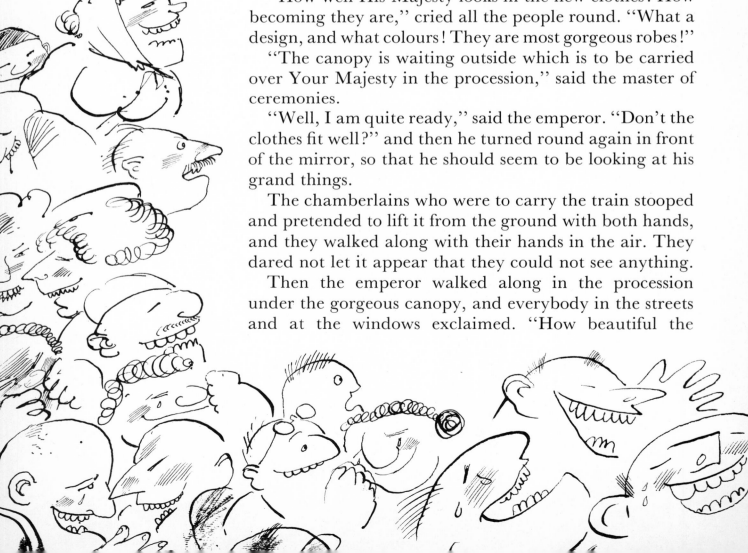

emperor's new clothes are! What a splendid train! And they fit to perfection!" Nobody would let it appear that he could see nothing, for then he would not be fit for his post, or else he was a fool.

None of the emperor's clothes had been so successful before.

"But he has got nothing on," said a little child.

"Oh, listen to the innocent," said its father; and one person whispered to the other what the child had said. "He has nothing on; a child says he has nothing on!"

"But he has nothing on!" at last cried all the people.

The emperor writhed, for he knew it was true, but he thought "The procession must go on now," so he held himself stiffer than ever, and the chamberlains held up the invisible train.

HANS CHRISTIAN ANDERSEN

The Ugly Duckling

The country was lovely just then; it was summer. The wheat was golden and the oats still green; the hay was stacked in the rich low-lying meadows, where the stork was marching about on his long red legs, chattering Egyptian, the language his mother had taught him.

Round about field and meadow lay great woods in the midst of which were deep lakes. Yes, the country certainly was delicious. In the sunniest spot stood an old mansion surrounded by a deep moat, and great dock leaves grew from the walls of the house right down to the water's edge; some of them were so tall that a small child could stand upright under them. In amongst the leaves it was as secluded as in the depths of a forest; and there a duck was sitting on her nest. Her little ducklings were just about to be hatched, but she was nearly tired of sitting, for it had lasted such a long time. Moreover, she had very few visitors, as the other ducks liked swimming about in the moat better than waddling up to sit under the dock leaves and gossip with her.

At last one egg after another began to crack. "Cheep, cheep!" they said. All the chicks had come to life, and were poking their heads out.

"Quack, quack!" said the ducks; and then they all quacked their hardest, and looked about them on all sides among the green leaves; their mother allowed them to look as much as they liked, for green is good for the eyes.

"How big the world is to be sure!" said all the young ones; for they certainly had ever so much more room to move about, than when they were inside in the eggshell.

"Do you imagine this is the whole world?" said the mother. "It stretches a long way on the other side of the garden, right into the parson's field; but I have never been as far as that. I suppose you are all here now?" and she got up. "No! I declare I have not got you all yet. The biggest egg is still there; how long is it going to last?" and then she settled herself on the nest again.

"Well, how are you getting on?" said an old duck who had come to pay her a visit.

"This one egg is taking such a long time," answered the sitting duck, "the shell will not crack; but now you must look at the others; they are the finest ducklings I have ever seen! they are all exactly like their father, the rascal! he never comes to see me."

"Let me look at the egg which won't crack," said the old duck. "You may be sure that it is a turkey's egg! I have been cheated like that once, and I had no end of trouble and worry with the creatures, for I may tell you that they are afraid of the water. I could not get them into it. I quacked and snapped at them, but it was no good. Let me see the egg! Yes, it is a turkey's egg! You just leave it alone and teach the other children to swim."

"I will sit on it a little longer. I have sat so long already, that I may as well go on till the Midsummer Fair comes round."

"Please yourself," said the old duck, and she went away.

At last the big egg cracked. "Cheep, cheep!" said the young one and tumbled out; how big and ugly he was!

The duck looked at him.

"That is a monstrous big duckling," she said; "none of the others looked like that; can he be a turkey chick? Well, we shall soon find that out; into the water he shall go, if I have to kick him in myself."

Next day was gloriously fine, and the sun shone on all the green dock leaves. The mother duck with her whole family went down to the moat.

Splash, into the water she sprang. "Quack, quack!" she said, and one duckling plumped in after the other. The water dashed over their heads, but they came up again and floated beautifully; their legs went of themselves, and they were all there, even the big ugly grey one swam about with them.

"No, that is no turkey," she said; "see how beautifully he uses his legs and how erect he holds himself; he is my own chick! After all, he is not so bad when you come to look at him properly. Quack, quack! Now come with me and I will take you into the world, and introduce you to the duckyard; but keep close to me all the time, so that no one may tread upon you, and beware of the cat!"

Then they went into the duckyard. There was a fearful uproar going on, for two broods were fighting for the head of an eel, and in the end the cat captured it.

"That's how things go in this world," said the mother duck, and she licked her bill for she wanted the eel's head herself.

"Use your legs," said she; "mind you quack properly, and bend your necks to the old duck over there! She is the grandest of them all; she has Spanish blood in her veins and that accounts for her size, and, do you see? she has a red rag round her leg; that is a wonderfully fine thing, and the most extraordinary mark of distinction any duck can have. It shows clearly that she is not to be parted with,

and that she is worthy of recognition both by beasts and men! Quack now! don't turn your toes in, a well-brought-up duckling keeps his legs wide apart just like father and mother; that's it, now bend your necks, and say quack."

They did as they were bid, but the other ducks round about looked at them and said, quite loud: "Just look there! now we are to have that tribe! just as if there were not enough of us already, and, oh dear! how ugly that duckling is, we won't stand him!" and a duck flew at him at once and bit him in the neck.

"Let him be," said the mother; "he is doing no harm."

"Very likely not, but he is so ungainly and queer," said the biter; "he must be whacked."

"They are handsome children mother has," said the old duck with the rag round her leg; "all good-looking except this one, and he is not a good specimen; it's a pity you can't make him over again."

"That can't be done, your grace," said the mother duck; "he is not handsome, but he is a thorough good creature, and he swims as beautifully as any of the others; nay, I think I might venture even to add that I think he will improve as he goes on, or perhaps in time he may grow smaller! he was too long in the egg, and so he has not come out with a very good figure." And then she patted his neck and stroked him down. "Besides he is a drake," said she; "so it does not matter so much. I believe he will be very strong, and I don't doubt but he will make his way in the world."

"The other ducklings are very pretty," said the old duck. "Now make yourselves quite at home, and if you find the head of an eel you may bring it to me!"

After that they felt quite at home. But the poor duckling which had been the last to come out of the shell, and who was so ugly, was bitten, pushed about, and made fun of

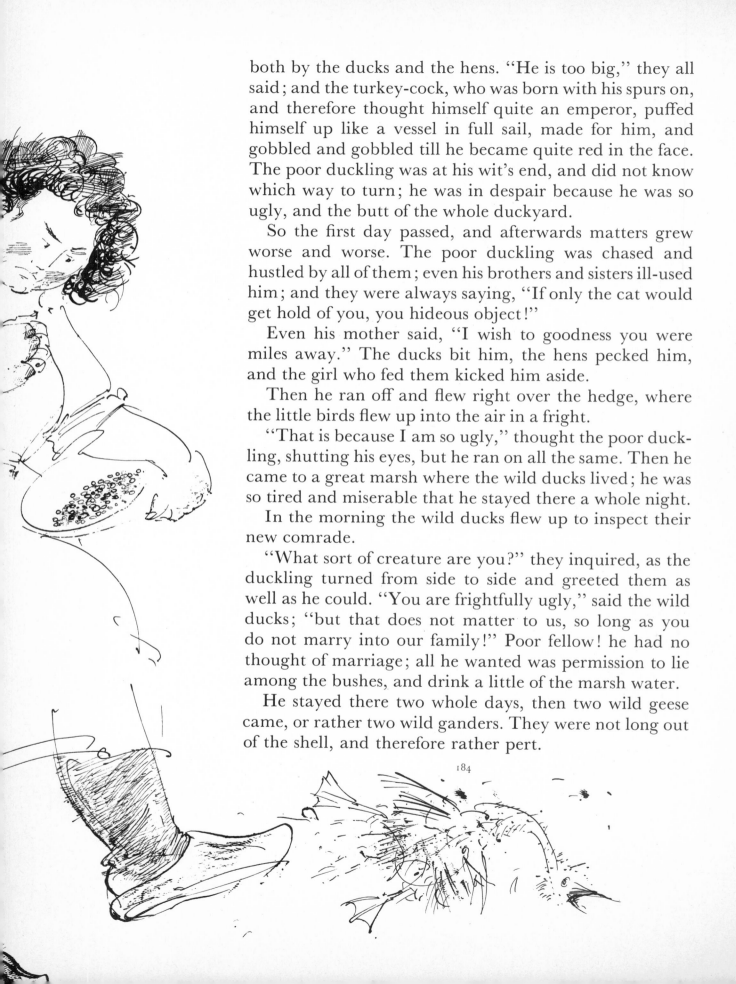

both by the ducks and the hens. "He is too big," they all said; and the turkey-cock, who was born with his spurs on, and therefore thought himself quite an emperor, puffed himself up like a vessel in full sail, made for him, and gobbled and gobbled till he became quite red in the face. The poor duckling was at his wit's end, and did not know which way to turn; he was in despair because he was so ugly, and the butt of the whole duckyard.

So the first day passed, and afterwards matters grew worse and worse. The poor duckling was chased and hustled by all of them; even his brothers and sisters ill-used him; and they were always saying, "If only the cat would get hold of you, you hideous object!"

Even his mother said, "I wish to goodness you were miles away." The ducks bit him, the hens pecked him, and the girl who fed them kicked him aside.

Then he ran off and flew right over the hedge, where the little birds flew up into the air in a fright.

"That is because I am so ugly," thought the poor duckling, shutting his eyes, but he ran on all the same. Then he came to a great marsh where the wild ducks lived; he was so tired and miserable that he stayed there a whole night.

In the morning the wild ducks flew up to inspect their new comrade.

"What sort of creature are you?" they inquired, as the duckling turned from side to side and greeted them as well as he could. "You are frightfully ugly," said the wild ducks; "but that does not matter to us, so long as you do not marry into our family!" Poor fellow! he had no thought of marriage; all he wanted was permission to lie among the bushes, and drink a little of the marsh water.

He stayed there two whole days, then two wild geese came, or rather two wild ganders. They were not long out of the shell, and therefore rather pert.

"I say, comrade," they said, "you are so ugly that we have taken quite a fancy to you; will you join us and be a bird of passage? There is another marsh close by, and there are some charming wild geese there, all sweet young ladies, who can say quack! You are ugly enough to make your fortune among them." Just at that moment, bang! bang! was heard up above, and both the wild geese fell dead among the reeds, and the water turned blood red. Bang! bang! went the guns, and whole flocks of wild geese flew up from the rushes and the shot peppered among them again.

There was a grand shooting party, and the sportsmen lay hidden round the marsh, some even sat on the branches of the trees which overhung the water; the blue smoke rose like clouds among the dark trees and swept over the pool.

The water-dogs wandered about in the swamp, splash! splash! The rushes and reeds bent beneath their tread on all sides. It was terribly alarming to the poor duckling. He twisted his head round to get it under his wing and just at that moment a big dog appeared close beside him; his tongue hung right out of his mouth and his eyes glared wickedly. He opened his great chasm of a mouth close to the duckling, showed his sharp teeth – and – splash – went on without touching him.

"Oh, thank Heaven!" sighed the duckling. "I am so ugly that even the dog won't bite me."

Then he lay quite still while the shot whistled among the bushes, and bang after bang rent the air. It only became quiet late in the day, but even then the poor duckling did not dare to get up; he waited several hours more before he looked about and then he hurried away from the marsh as fast as he could. He ran across fields and meadows, and there was such a wind that he had hard work to make his way.

Towards night he reached a poor little cottage; it was such a miserable hovel that it could not make up its mind which way to fall even, and so it remained standing. The wind whistled so fiercely round the duckling that he had to sit on his tail to resist it, and it blew harder and harder; then he saw that the door had fallen off one hinge and hung so crookedly that he could creep into the house through the crack and by this means he made his way into the room. An old woman lived there with her cat and her hen. The cat, which she called "Sonnie", could arch his back, purr, and give off electric sparks, that is to say if you stroked his fur the wrong way. The hen had quite tiny short legs and so she was called "Chuckie-low-legs". She laid good eggs, and the old woman was as fond of her as if she had been her own child.

In the morning the strange duckling was discovered immediately, and the cat began to purr and the hen to cluck.

"What on earth is that!" said the old woman looking round, but her sight was not good and she thought the duckling was a fat duck which had escaped. "This is a capital find," said she; "now I shall have duck's eggs if only it is not a drake! we must find out about that!"

So she took the duckling on trial for three weeks, but no eggs made their appearance. The cat was the master of the house and the hen the mistress, and they always spoke of "we and the world", for they thought that they represented the half of the world, and that quite the better half.

The duckling thought there might be two opinions on the subject, but the hen would not hear of it.

"Can you lay eggs?" she asked.

"No!"

"Will you have the goodness to hold your tongue then!"

And the cat said:

"Can you arch your back, purr, or give off sparks?"

"No."

"Then you had better keep your opinions to yourself when people of sense are speaking!"

The duckling sat in the corner nursing his ill-humour; then he began to think of the fresh air and the sunshine, an uncontrollable longing seized him to float on the water, and at last he could not help telling the hen about it.

"What on earth possesses you?" she asked; "You have nothing to do, that is why you get these freaks into your head. Lay some eggs or take to purring, and you will get over it."

"But it is so delicious to float on the water," said the duckling; "so delicious to feel it rushing over your head when you dive to the bottom."

"That would be a fine amusement," said the hen. "I think you have gone mad. Ask the cat about it, he is the wisest creature I know; ask him if he is fond of floating on the water or diving under it. I say nothing about myself. Ask our mistress yourself, the old woman, there is no one in the world cleverer than she is. Do you suppose she has any desire to float on the water, or to duck underneath it?"

"You do not understand me," said the duckling.

"Well, if we don't understand you, who should? I suppose you don't consider yourself cleverer than the cat or the old woman, not to mention me. Don't make a fool of yourself, child, and thank your stars for all the good we have done you! Have you not lived in this warm room, and in such society that you might have learnt something? But you are an idiot, and there is no pleasure in associating with you. You may believe me I mean you well, I tell you home truths, and there is no surer way than that, of knowing who are one's friends. You just see about laying some

eggs, or learn to purr, or to emit sparks."

"I think I will go out into the wide world," said the duckling.

"Oh, do so by all means," said the hen.

So away went the duckling. He floated on the water and ducked underneath it, but he was looked askance at by every living creature for his ugliness. Now the autumn came on, the leaves in the woods turned yellow and brown; the wind took hold of them, and they danced about. The sky looked very cold, and the clouds hung heavy with snow and hail. A raven stood on the fence and croaked Caw! Caw! from sheer cold; it made one shiver only to think of it, the poor duckling certainly was in a bad case.

One evening, the sun was just setting in wintry splendour, when a flock of beautiful large birds appeared out of the bushes; the duckling had never seen anything so beautiful. They were dazzlingly white with long waving necks; they were swans, and uttering a peculiar cry they spread out their magnificent broad wings and flew away from the cold regions to warmer lands and open seas. They mounted so high, so very high, and the ugly duckling became strangely uneasy, he circled round and round in the water like a wheel, craning his neck up into the air after them. Then he uttered a shriek so piercing and so strange, that he was quite frightened by it himself. Oh, he could not forget those beautiful birds, those happy birds, and as soon as they were out of sight he ducked right down to the bottom, and when he came up again he was quite beside himself. He did not know what the birds were, or whither they flew, but all the same he was more drawn towards them than he had ever been by any creatures before. He did not envy them in the least, how could it occur to him even to wish to be such a marvel of beauty;

he would have been thankful if only the ducks would have tolerated him among them – the poor ugly creature!

The winter was so bitterly cold that the duckling was obliged to swim about in the water to keep it from freezing, but every night the hole in which he swam got smaller and smaller. Then it froze so hard that the surface ice cracked, and the duckling had to use his legs all the time, so that the ice should not close in round him: at last he was so weary that he could move no more, and he was frozen fast into the ice.

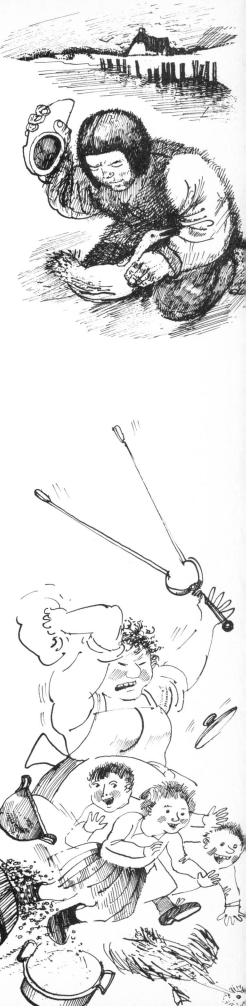

Early in the morning a peasant came along and saw him; he went out on to the ice and hammered a hole in it with his heavy wooden shoe, and carried the duckling home to his wife. There he soon revived. The children wanted to play with him, but the duckling thought they were going to ill-use him, and rushed in his fright into the milk pan, and the milk spurted out all over the room. The woman shrieked and threw up her hands, then he flew into the butter cask, and down into the meal tub and out again. Just imagine what he looked like by this time! The woman screamed and tried to hit him with the tongs, and the children tumbled over one another in trying to catch him, and they screamed with laughter – by good luck the door stood open, and the duckling flew out among the bushes and the new fallen snow – and he lay there thoroughly exhausted.

But it would be too sad to mention all the privation and misery he had to go through during that hard winter. When the sun began to shine warmly again, the duckling was in the marsh, lying among the rushes, the larks were singing and the beautiful spring had come.

Then all at once he raised his wings and they flapped with much greater strength than before, and bore him off vigorously. Before he knew where he was, he found himself in a large garden where the apple trees were in full blossom, and the air was scented with lilacs, the long branches of which overhung the indented shores of the lake! Oh! the spring freshness was so delicious!

Just in front of him he saw three beautiful white swans advancing towards him from a thicket; with rustling feathers they swam lightly over the water. The duckling recognized the majestic birds, and he was overcome by a strange melancholy.

"I will fly to them, the royal birds, and they will hack me to pieces, because I, who am so ugly, venture to approach them! But it won't matter; better be killed by them than be snapped at by the ducks, pecked by the hens, or spurned by the henwife, or suffer so much misery in the winter."

So he flew into the water and swam towards the stately swans; they saw him and darted towards him with ruffled feathers.

"Kill me, oh, kill me!" said the poor creature, and bowing his head towards the water he awaited his death. But what did he see reflected in the transparent water?

He saw below him his own image, but he was no longer a clumsy dark grey bird, ugly and ungainly, he was himself a swan! It does not matter in the least having been born in a duckyard, if only you come out of a swan's egg!

He felt quite glad of all the misery and tribulation he had gone through; he was the better able to appreciate his good fortune now, and all the beauty which greeted him. The big swans swam round and round him, and stroked him with their bills.

Some little children came into the garden with corn and pieces of bread, which they threw into the water; and the smallest one cried out: "There is a new one!" The other children shouted with joy. "Yes, a new one has come!" And they clapped their hands and danced about, running after their father and mother. They threw the bread into the water, and one and all said that the new one was the prettiest; he was so young and handsome. And the old swans bent their heads and did homage before him.

He felt quite shy, and hid his head under his wing; he did not know what to think; he was so very happy, but not at all proud; a good heart never becomes proud. He thought of how he had been pursued and scorned, and now he heard them all say that he was the most beautiful of all beautiful birds. The lilacs bent their boughs right down into the water before him, and the bright sun was warm and cheering, and he rustled his feathers and raised his slender neck aloft, saying with exultation in his heart: "I never dreamt of so much happiness when I was the Ugly Duckling!"

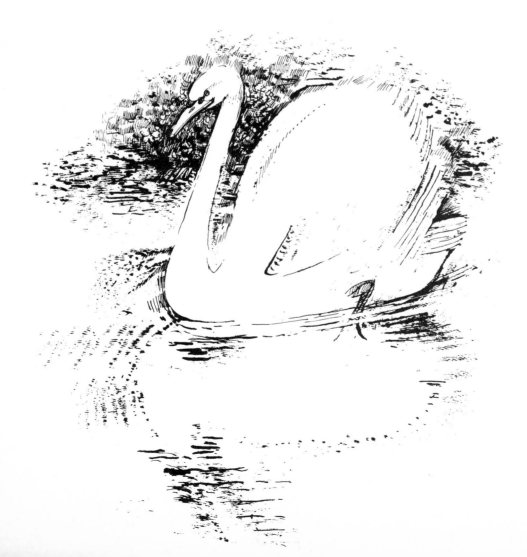

Acknowledgements

The Publishers are grateful to the following copyright holders for permission to include copyright material in this volume:

Coward McCann & Geoghegan, Inc., New York, for permission to include the text of GONE IS GONE by Wanda Gág. Copyright 1935 by Wanda Gág; copyright renewed 1963 by Robert Janssen. GONE IS GONE is published in Great Britain by Faber & Faber.

Macmillan, London, and The Macmillan Company, New York, for permission to include *The Story of the Three Bears* from ENGLISH FAIRY TALES by Flora Annie Steel.

Macmillan, London, and Thomas Y. Crowell, New York, for permission to include *From Tiger to Anansi* from ANANSI THE SPIDER MAN by Philip M. Sherlock.

Routledge & Kegan Paul Ltd., London, for permission to include *The Turnip* from RUSSIAN TALES FOR CHILDREN by Aleksei Tolstoy.

Longman & Company, London and New York, for permission to include *Wakaima and the Clay Man* from WAKAIMA AND THE CLAY MAN by Ernest Balintuma Kalibala and Mary Gould Davis. This is a story of the Baganda tribe of East Africa.

Houghton Mifflin Company, Boston, for permission to include *The Gingerbread Boy, The Little Red Hen and the Grain of Wheat* and *The Sun and the Wind* from STORIES TO TELL TO CHILDREN by Sara Cone Bryant.

Harcourt Brace Jovanovich, Inc., New York, for permission to include *Budulinek* from THE SHEPHERD'S NOSEGAY by Parker Fillmore, edited by Katherine Love. Copyright 1920 by Parker Fillmore, renewed 1948 by Louise Fillmore.

J. B. Lippincott Company, Philadelphia, for permission to include *One Inch Fellow* from PICTURE TALES FROM THE JAPANESE by Chiyono Sugimoto. Copyright 1928 by F. A. Stokes Co. Renewal © 1956 by Mrs. Chiyono Sugimoto Kiyooka. The version in THE FAIRY TALE TREASURY has been retold by Virginia Haviland, © 1967, and was first published in FAVOURITE FAIRY TALES TOLD IN JAPAN, Little, Brown & Company, Boston; The Bodley Head, London.

The Publishers are particularly grateful for the help and co-operation received from Little, Brown and Company, Boston, who have granted permission for the use of the following material: *Rumpel-stiltskin, The Elves and the Shoemaker, The Frog Prince* and *The Bremen Town Musicians,* all translated from the original German of the Brothers Grimm and retold by Virginia Haviland in FAVOURITE FAIRY TALES TOLD IN GERMANY, © 1959 by Virginia Haviland; *The Half-Chick,* adapted from *Little Half-Chick* in THE GREEN FAIRY BOOK by Andrew Lang and retold by Virginia Haviland in FAVOURITE FAIRY TALES TOLD IN SPAIN, © 1963 by Virginia Haviland; *Tom Thumb, Molly Whuppie* and *Jack and the Beanstalk,* retold by Virginia Haviland from Joseph Jacobs in FAVOURITE FAIRY TALES TOLD IN ENGLAND, © 1959 by Virginia Haviland; *Puss in Boots,* translated and retold from the original French version by Charles Perrault by Virginia Haviland in FAVOURITE FAIRY TALES TOLD IN FRANCE, © 1959 by Virginia Haviland.

The FAVOURITE FAIRY TALE Books by Virginia Haviland are published in the United States of America by Little, Brown & Company, Boston, and in Great Britain by The Bodley Head, London. The following stories have been retold and first published in this volume: *Snow-white,* retold from the Lucy Crane translation of the story by the Brothers Grimm by Virginia Haviland, © 1972 Virginia Haviland; *Little Red Riding-Hood,* translated and retold from Charles Perrault by Virginia Haviland, © 1972 Virginia Haviland; *Cinderella,* retold from the version in Andrew Lang's BLUE FAIRY BOOK by Virginia Haviland, © 1972 Virginia Haviland.

Unless otherwise stated the translations of the stories by Hans Andersen are by Mrs. E. Lucas, and the translations of the stories by the Brothers Grimm are by Lucy Crane. Translation of the story by Asbjörnsen and Moe is by Sir George Webb Dasent.